ALSO BY VLADIMIR NABOKOV

THE TRAGEDY
of
MR MORN

THE TRAGEDY of MR MORN

BY

VLADIMIR NABOKOV

WITH AN INTRODUCTION BY THOMAS KARSHAN

TRANSLATION BY ANASTASIA TOLSTOY AND THOMAS KARSHAN

ALFRED A. KNOPF NEW YORK 2013

THIS IS A BORZOI BOOK
PUBLISHED BY ALFRED A. KNOPF

Introduction copyright © 2012 by Thomas Karshan
Translation copyright © 2012 by Thomas Karshan and Anastasia Tolstoy

Illustrations by Pablo Delcán

www.aaknopf.com

Originally serialized in Russian, in somewhat different form,
in *Zvezda* (1997).

Library of Congress Cataloguing-in-Publication Data
Nabokov, Vladimir Vladimirovich, 1899–1977.
[Tragediia gospodina Morna. English]
The tragedy of Mister Morn / by Vladimir Nabokov ;
with an introduction by Thomas Karshan ;
translation by Anastasia Tolstoy and Thomas Karshan.
p. cm.
"This is a Borzoi book."
ISBN 978-0-307-96081-8
I. Tolstoy, Anastasia.   II. Karshan, Thomas.   III. Title.
IV. Title: Tragedy of Mister Morn.
PG3476.N3T8313 2013
891.72'42—dc23   2012037121

Jacket design by Pablo Delcán

Manufactured in the United States of America
First United States Edition

CONTENTS

INTRODUCTION

The Tragedy of Mister Morn was Vladimir Nabokov's first major work, and the laboratory in which he discovered and tested many of the themes he would subsequently develop in the next fifty-odd years: the elusiveness of happiness; the creative and destructive playfulness of the imagination; courage, cowardice, and loyalty; the truth of masks; the struggle of freedom and order for possession of the soul; the sovereignty of desire and illicit passion; and what one character calls "that likeness which exists/between truth and high fantasy" (I.ii.59–60), a likeness under whose inspiration Nabokov would take reality, fancy, art, and impossibility, and twist them together into the four-dimensional knots of *Lolita*, *Pale Fire*, and his other great novels.

Yet *Morn*, which Nabokov wrote in Prague in the winter of 1923 to 1924, when he was only twenty-four years old, was never performed or published in his lifetime, though several readings of the play did take place in Berlin, then Nabokov's home, in the spring of 1923. The opportunities in Berlin for staging a Russian play by a nearly unknown writer were limited, and publication cannot have seemed financially attractive to the émigré publishing houses that would later print Nabokov's novels. In America, and then in Switzerland, Nabokov translated most of his Russian fiction, but not his early plays, and when he died, in 1977, the typescript and fair copy of *Morn* still lay dormant in his personal archive in Montreux. Then, in 1997, *Zvezda*, a Russian literary journal, published the complete Russian text of *Morn*; and in 2008 the play finally became available to a wider (Russian-reading) audience when a revised version of the text was published in book form by Azbuka Press of St. Petersburg. These publications have in turn made possible this current edition—the first translation of *Morn* into English.

While *Morn* is in many respects the seedbed for Nabokov's major novels, there are also elements in it which are fascinatingly unlike anything in his later work, and which reflect issues in Nabokov's life at the time of writing. Most prominent of these is revolution. Nabokov came from a distinguished liberal family in St. Petersburg: his father, V. D. Nabokov, had been one of the ministers in the short-lived Kerensky government which ruled between the fall of the Tsar and the ascent to power of Lenin and the Bolsheviks in 1917. That year, the Nabokov family fled St. Petersburg, first for Yalta, then for London, and, eventually, Berlin—where the young Nabokov would rejoin them in 1922, after completing his degree at Cambridge. Even in Berlin, however, the Nabokov family was not safe from the extremist ideologies of right and left which had vied for power in Russia after the failure of the liberal centre, and on March 28, 1922, Nabokov's father was shot dead by a Monarchist assassin who was in fact aiming not at him but at another émigré politician.

Nabokov's hatred of the Soviet regime is directly expressed in much of his writing, most prominently his novels *Invitation to a Beheading* (1935–36) and *Bend Sinister* (1947). But he would never again write anywhere nearly so directly about the moment of revolution itself, or so probingly about ideology, as he did in *Morn*. In the play's two main revolutionaries, Tremens and Klian, Nabokov depicts a politics and poetics of nihilism which, it is implied, was the driving force behind the Russian Revolution. In this Nabokov was refining a critique of revolutionary ideology which can be traced back as far as Turgenev's *Fathers and Sons* (1862) and Dostoevsky's *The Possessed* (1872). He would articulate this critique again in his last, and greatest, Russian novel, *The Gift* (1937–38), whose fourth chapter is a mocking biography of Nikolai Chernyshevsky—the revolutionary thinker of the 1860s who was the object of Turgenev's and Dostoevsky's conservative critiques, and would become Lenin's hero. But in *Morn* Nabokov explores more fully and explicitly than he ever would again what he saw as the origins of the revolutionary impulse in a death-instinct and passion for destruction. When Ganus, who had once been a revolutionary, returns from exile and discovers the happiness that the masked King has brought to the kingdom, he asks Tremens why he is not now satisfied. Tremens pours scorn on him. Neither happiness nor equality is Tremens's purpose, he explains; rather, he is seeking to imitate the violent destructiveness of life itself, which "rushes headlong/ into ash, [and] destroys everything in its way" (I.i.287–88). "Everything," Tremens explains, "is destruction. And/the faster it is, the sweeter, the sweeter . . ." (I.i.295–96). To him, this destruction is beauty:

> Did you see,
> one windy night, by moonlight, the shadows
> of ruins? That is the ultimate beauty—
> and towards it I lead the world.
>   (I.i.267–70)

Tremens cites as one aspect of that destructiveness the sexual drive itself, in the figure of "the maiden, who prays for the blow of a man's love" (I.i.294), and one distinctive quality of the play is an unblushing erotic candour to which Nabokov would not fully return until *Lolita* (1955). Thus Klian, the violent-minded revolutionary poet who serves as Tremens's factotum, tells his fiancée Ella that

> . . . To enter you, oh, to enter,
> would be like entering a tight and searing
> sheath, to gaze into your blood, to break
> through your bones, to learn, to grasp, to touch,
> to press your being in between my palms! . . .
> (I.ii.122–26)

This anticipates Humbert Humbert in Chapter 2, Part Two of *Lolita* saying that "my only grudge against nature was that I could not turn my Lolita inside out and apply voracious lips to her young matrix, her unknown heart, her nacreous liver, the sea-grapes of her lungs, her comely twin kidneys." Yet, as with so many aspects of the play, in the sphere of desire Nabokov explores opposite poles of experience. Against Klian's dark vision of sexual appetite is set a more salubrious expression of love's idealizing power—in the faith that Midia, and the other citizens, place in Morn's nearly magical beneficence, and in Ella's idea of love as a force that coalesces experience:

> . . . all is one: my love and the raw sun,
> your pale face and the bright trickling icicles
> beneath the roof, the amber spot upon
> the porous sugary snow mound, the raw sun
> and my love, my love . . .
> (III.ii.190–94)

This, and the tenderly specific attention paid to the minutiae of Ella's hair, clothes, and make-up, seem to attest to the fact that Nabokov wrote *Morn* soon after meeting and falling in love with Véra Slonim, who would become his wife—and the play's typist. With her girlishness, humour, and idealism, Ella ranks alongside Lolita as one of Nabokov's few fully realized female characters.

If, in its treatment of revolutionary ideology, death, and desire,

Morn shows us elements that Nabokov would not develop again, or not for a long time, there is one respect in which it stands very obviously as the source of Nabokov's immediately subsequent writing, and this is in its exploration of the twin themes of happiness and make-believe. In 1924, Nabokov would begin writing his first novel, *Happiness*. The novel was aborted and its drafts are now lost, but there is no question that its title expresses one of the central themes of Nabokov's oeuvre, in which happiness is a mysterious variable, "the zany of its own mortality," as Sebastian Knight calls it, no sooner found than lost, but always something much more profound than anything "happiness" means in modern use, where it merely names the mirage evoked by the goals we set ourselves. As for make-believe, it is central to Nabokov's work that any reality worth caring about is one freshly imagined, that, as he puts it in *Strong Opinions* (1973), "average reality begins to rot and stink as soon as the act of individual creation ceases to animate a subjectively perceived texture," and therefore that, as Vadim's aunt tells him in Chapter 2 of Nabokov's final complete novel, *Look at the Harlequins!* (1974), it is a fundamental imperative for every person that in art and life he should "Play! Invent the world! Create it!" The theme of make-believe also links *Morn* to two other verse-plays which Nabokov had written in 1923 before embarking on *Morn*, the one-act closet dramas *Death* and *The Pole*, which together mark out the two poles between which *Morn* moves: in the first, a cynical intellectual related in mentality to Tremens presses the view of illusion as arrant deceit; while the second heroizes Captain Scott, the quixotic Antarctic explorer, a Morn-like figure whose steadfast courage inspires and sustains his followers, who always seems to be playing, even in the face of death, and who is, like Morn, recognized by his laughter.

In *Morn* Nabokov gave these themes a political significance more explicit than any we find in his later work. Against the revolutionary politics, grounded in the ideals of equality, sameness, and even death, that Tremens and Klian embody, Nabokov postulates a conservative politics, animated by an ideal of happiness. As Morn says, he

>   . . . created
> an age of happiness, an age of harmony . . . God,
> give me strength . . . Playfully, lightly I ruled;
> I appeared in a black mask in the ringing hall,
> before my cold, decrepit senators . . . masterfully
> I revived them—and left again, laughing . . .
>   (III.i.131–36)

Morn's example has aestheticized the world, restoring order by turning it into a fairy tale or a play: if even the King is an actor, then all identity is not something sovereign but something performed, and he shows people how to act as they would wish to be. He is a fantasy of the Foreigner, a mysterious figure who enters at the beginning and the end of the play and comes from the real world of revolutionary Russia:

>   . . . In our country all is not well,
> not well . . . When I wake up, I will tell them
> what a magnificent king I dreamt of . . .
>   (V.ii.98–100)

The implicit argument of *Morn* is that for the sake of order, morality, and happiness in the real world, people must make-believe in the possibility of an ideal world. The play takes place in an imaginary kingdom repeatedly described as having the air of a *skazka* or fairy tale. In a synopsis of the play, Nabokov described this atmosphere as "neoromanticism," saying that the setting of the play took "something from the 18th Century Venice of Casanova and from the 30s [the 1830s] of the Petersburg epoch." It also borrows from Shakespeare, for in *Morn*, as in Shakespeare's history plays such as *Richard III*, the state is, necessarily, a play or pageant; a secret passage leads from the throne-room to the theatre. This is one of the many details that Nabokov would reuse nearly forty years later in his most metafictive work, *Pale Fire* (1962), in which an imaginary poet and imaginary king conjure with each other's existences. Kinbote, the imaginary King of Zembla, or semblance, may have assassinated Shade, the imaginary poet, just as in *Morn* Tremens says: "it's a shame, Dandilio, that the imaginary / thief did not destroy the made-up king!" (V.i.188–89). But in *Morn*, as later in *Pale Fire*, this kingdom of imagination is all too precarious: Tremens is determined to unmask Morn's happy reign of make-believe as a cynical fraud, and to tear down the civic order it supports. He succeeds in doing so, until a false rumour that Morn fled for love, not cowardice, reignites the romanticism of the people. It is to defend that illusion that Morn, ultimately, must kill himself.

This idea of kingship as theatre, or as a work of imagination, is one of the many respects in which *Morn* is indebted to Shakespeare. The heavy crown is a symbol of the burdensomeness of power, as it is in Shakespeare's history plays, such as *Henry IV, Part 2*, towards the end of which Prince Henry stares uneasily at the crown lying on his dying father's pillow, "so troublesome a bedfellow," which, he says, "dost pinch thy bearer," and "dost sit / Like a rich armour worn in heat of day, / That scalds with safety" (IV.v.22, 29–31). In *Morn*, too, the "fiery crown" burns and squeezes with "its diamond pain," and Morn complains that

> . . . The stupefied mob
> does not know that the knight's body is dark
> and sweaty, locked in its fairy tale armour . . .
> (V.ii.124–26)

From Shakespeare, too, Nabokov drew a series of metaphors for civic order which could be deployed to warn against the rash alterations of Bolshevism. The kingdom is like the human body, so that Tremens's fever symbolizes the convulsions he wishes upon the state, as, again, in *Henry IV, Part 2*, where the Archbishop of York declares that

> . . . we are all diseased,
> And with our surfeiting and wanton hours
> Have brought ourselves into a burning fever,
> And we must bleed for it.
> (IV.i.54–57)

Or the kingdom is like music, as Ganus argues when he says that "The power of the King / is living and harmonious, it moves me now / like music" (I.i.231–33), echoing an idea most famously expressed in a speech given by Ulysses in Shakespeare's *Troilus and Cressida*. The same idea is implicit in *The Tempest*, a play with which *Morn* is associated through the kinship between Prospero and Morn, both of them magician-kings. But the Shakespeare play most obviously linked to *Morn* is *Othello*: Ella dresses Ganus up as Othello so that he can visit Midia unobserved, and she twice quotes the lines Desdemona utters when Othello is about to smother her (the first time slightly misquoting them). *The Tragedy of Mister Morn* is less concerned with doubling, and with the duality of human nature, than Nabokov's later works. But here already, it is clear that when Ganus wears Othello's face, he discovers in himself a shadow side, a dark jealousy like that which blackened and distorted Othello. Conversely, Morn, by wearing a mask, becomes a nameless sovereign, King X, as Nabokov calls him in the synopsis, the variable upon which a lucky people can project their fantasies of happiness and order; and when he is unmasked by his cowardice, he betrays not only the ideals of his people and his own self-respect but even the identity and integrity he had once seen when he gazed into the healing silver of the mirror.

But in *Morn* Nabokov was trying to emulate Shakespeare not only at the level of image and symbol, but also of character and drama, register and rhythm. The simplest expression of this is that *Morn* is written in the iambic pentameter of Shakespearean tragedy, though Nabokov is more strictly regular in his rhythmic patterns than Shakespeare. Though *Morn*'s prosody alludes to Shakespeare, it does so through the mediation of Pushkin's "little tragedies" (all written in 1830, the most famous of which is *Mozart and Salieri*). More specifically Shakespearean—and un-Pushkinian—is the language of *Morn*, which, especially in the philosophic speeches of Tremens, Klian, Morn and Dandilio, is densely metaphorical and highly compressed in the manner of late Shakespeare. So Morn, saying farewell to Midia, justifies the aberrations of fate by comparing life to music, before suddenly shifting the already difficult metaphor into another key, comparing the music of existence to the structure of a building whose details can detract from an appreciation of its overall harmony:

> But, you see—the moulded whimsy of a frieze
> on a portico keeps us from recognizing,
> sometimes, the symmetry of the whole . . .
> (IV.235–37)

Or Dandilio compares moments of life, good and bad, to pearls which a deep-sea diver must clutch up indiscriminately in his brief breathless moments at the bottom of the ocean, and pursues the metaphor to a visionary limit far beyond any which the mind can easily grasp:

> And he who seeks only pearls, setting aside
> shell after shell, that man shall come to
> the Creator, to the Master, with empty hands—
> and he will find that he is deaf and dumb
> in heaven . . .
>   (I.ii.38–42)

The conceits are often as whimsical as those in Shakespeare, defying that Enlightenment ideal of rhetorical decorum according to which Shakespeare's imagination was deplored as savage and untutored. So Tremens declares that

> . . . The soul is like a tooth, God
> wrenches out the soul—crunch!—and it is over . . .
> What comes next? Unthinkable nausea and then—
> the void, spirals of madness—and the feeling of being
> a swirling spermatozoid—and then darkness,
> darkness—the velvety abyss of the grave . . .
>   (II.208–13)

Or, earlier, he remembers an evening in which he "shook with fever, / rippling like a reflection in an ice-hole" (I.i.93–94). One is reminded of a line in Chapter 26 of Nabokov's penultimate novel, *Transparent Things*, which was finished nearly fifty years after *Morn*, in 1972, about "an African nun in an arctic convent touching with delight the fragile clock of her first dandelion." Such wild conceits, yoking together hot fancy and cold reason, are common in Nabokov's mature style. They derive, as *Morn* helps us to see, from Shakespeare, and mark the rebellion of Nabokov's genius against the decorousness of the Age of Reason.

Equally Shakespearean is Nabokov's subtly reasoned orchestration of many different voices and registers. At one extreme, we have the high-toned rhetoric of Tremens, Klian, Morn, Dandilio, and Ganus, each of whom Nabokov endows with an individual voice that speaks of their desires, values, and condition. The first note struck is that of Tremens's feverish rhetoric, tightly coiled upon itself, thickly patterned with spite and self-pity, and embroidered with antique curses: "Begone, fever, you snake!" (I.i.7). In Klian, the court poet of Tremens's revolution, that destructiveness finds a sexual urgency which takes his rhetoric to the very limit of intelligibility. In our translation, we have allowed many of his speeches to remain as obscure in English as they are in the original Russian, where they seem to evince his commitment to the revolutionary poetics of violence upon the word associated with such poets as Vladimir Mayakovsky (1893–1930), on whom he may be modelled.

At the other pole of the play's rhetoric are Morn and Dandilio: in Morn there is a noble purity and simplicity of speech—"radiant," to identify it by one of Morn's own favourite words. Although Morn is not a poet, he has the champagne-like effervescence he himself identifies with creativity, and it is definitive of him that when Ganus attacks him he responds with the carefree laughter which gives him his power. Dandilio shares with Morn this equanimity, which is not to be mistaken for a Buddhist absence of will or desire: on the contrary, Dandilio urges that life be embraced without scruple or discrimination. He is a snuff-taking eighteenth-century Optimist of the kind Voltaire famously satirized in *Candide,* and whom Nabokov would reprise in the figure of *Pale Fire's* John Shade. He believes that all in the world is well, good and evil, Morn and Tremens alike. In the compressed aphorisms of his speeches the sententious gravity of the Age of Reason is combined with the intermittently childlike and sing-song tenor of its thought.

Indeed, memories of childhood, and especially of the pains and illnesses of childhood, stud the play, introducing into it a domestic counterpoint to the stagy rhetoric, in something like the way that Shakespeare typically sets tavern against court, and prose against verse. (The Old Man who enters to clean up after Edmin and Morn have fled is, with his rustic speech, closely reminiscent of such Shakespearean characters as the Porter in *Macbeth*.) Dandilio says that life assuages all pain, like a mother rushing in to kiss better a child who has scratched itself (II.340–45); Midia says her soul is attached to Morn like a child's tongue to the metal it has licked on a frosty day (I.ii.253–56); and the feel of a cold gun muzzle pressing up against his chest reminds Morn, at a moment when he is considering suicide, of the "lacquer tube" a doctor once pressed against his chest (III.i.119–22). In Ella that domesticity is articulated with a freshness that is essential to the total effect of the play, and it is telling that she often expresses herself in gestures—twirling, stroking the air—rather than in the destructive speechifying of Tremens, Klian, and Ganus.

As all of the above indicates, *Morn* presents some extraordinary difficulties to its translators. The task of translating it is all the more daunting because Nabokov was himself one of the most prominent modern critics of lazy and careless translation. As a young man, Nabokov had written elegant, readable translations of a range of English and French authors, from Carroll and Keats to Ronsard, Byron, and Shakespeare. In America, in the 1940s, he also produced verse translations into English of some of Pushkin's little tragedies, of Fyodor Tyutchev, Mikhail Lermontov, and Afanasy Fet. Yet he began to stress the near-impossibility of successful translation, describing it in Chapter 7 of his 1947 novel *Bend Sinister* by the following extravagant analogy:

> It was as if someone, having seen a certain oak tree (further called Individual T) growing in a certain land and casting its own unique shadow on the green and brown ground, had proceeded to erect in his garden a prodigiously intricate piece of machinery which

in itself was as unlike that or any other tree as the translator's inspiration and language were unlike those of the original author, but which, by means of ingenious combinations of parts, light effects, breeze-engendering engines, would, when completed, cast a shadow exactly similar to that of Individual T—the same outline, changing in the same manner, with the same double and single spots of suns rippling in the same position, at the same hour of the day.

Or, as he put it still more tersely, and (to a translator) intimidatingly, in his poem "On Translating 'Eugene Onegin'" (1955):

> What is translation? On a platter
> A poet's pale and glaring head,
> A parrot's screech, a monkey's chatter,
> And profanation of the dead.

That translation of Pushkin's *Eugene Onegin*, which was published in 1964 alongside three volumes of commentary, is famous, or notorious, for its defiant fidelity to rendering the exact and complete meaning of the original text at the expense of readability or elegance in English—a fidelity that Nabokov called "the servile path."

Our policy has been to prioritize accuracy to Nabokov's language, wherever possible, but we have not sought to produce a crib, as Nabokov did in his translation of *Eugene Onegin*. Rather we have aimed to find words, phrases, and rhythms which do justice both to the exact shades of meaning and to the very various tones and registers of Nabokov's *Morn*—and to finish with a text that re-creates at least some of the power and beauty of the original, both in private reading and in performance. Our goal has been to produce a text that does not sound like a translation, but like the play that Nabokov would have written had he written

Morn in English in 1923. That ideal is not entirely speculative, given that we do have some poems and essays which Nabokov wrote in English in the early 1920s, as well as the example of his own translations of his early Russian work into English, and his own writings in English. Nabokov read and wrote English from an early age, studied in Cambridge from 1919 to 1922, and was regarded by the other Russian émigrés as strongly oriented towards England and the English language. There are places in *Morn*, especially in the speeches of the title character, where the Russian hints of English—as, conversely, in *Pnin* and *Lolita*, Nabokov writes an English which sounds distinctly foreign. There are also many places in the text, and especially in Tremens's and Klian's speeches, where the Russian language is being deliberately wrenched into a revolutionary strangeness.

We have throughout resisted all temptations to tame or normalize Nabokov's language, which often sounds as distinctive and peculiar in Russian as in our translation—or, for that matter, as in Nabokov's own English. Indeed, there are moments in the text where we were able to draw on Nabokov's own translation of a phrase. So, for instance, when Midia has left Morn, he uses the curious phrase *letuchii dozhd'*—literally, "flying rain." We might have been tempted to make this "fleeting rain," were it not for the fact that one of Nabokov's first poems, from 1917, is entitled *"Dozhd' proletel,"* which Nabokov himself translated as "The Rain Has Flown," adding in a note printed in *Poems and Problems* (1970) that "The phrase *letit dozhd'*, 'rain is flying,' was borrowed by the author from an old gardener (described in *Speak, Memory*, Chapter 2 *et passim*) who applied it to light rain soon followed by sunshine." In the opening speech of the play, we have sought to preserve Tremens's warlock-like tones and his elliptical, highly compressed images. So, too, when Ella in the same scene addresses the coals burning in the fireplace, she uses a strange and archaic phrase—*"Chur—goret'!"*—which we have translated by a phrase equally strange and archaic: "Fain burn!" (I.i.39). In this case we were influenced by the modern associations of the word "fain" with Shakespeare. In his translation of Pushkin, Nabokov often sought out the phrases in such poets as Byron which Pushkin had reworked into Russian; we have done the same in trying to retain the shimmering pale fire of Shakespeare's language which is often glimpsed in Nabokov's original Russian. This Shakespeareanism is always dominant but it often in turn absorbs and transforms the echoes of other literary exemplars, so that in Dandilio the terse aphorisms of a Voltaire or a Pope acquire Shakespearean vividness and whimsy, a richness of imagery which, conversely, deepens the fractured, syntax-defying Futurist speeches of Klian. In short, the play contains a range of registers and discourses, often overlain, and we have had to try to reproduce this in our translation.

In a few, though not very many, instances, we have permitted ourselves to travel a fair way beyond the original Russian, where reproducing it would have resulted in entirely the wrong feel and tone, though always with the intention of expressing the essential meaning. In Act II, Tremens declares: *"Segodnia otkryvaiu/moi nebyvalyi prazdnik"*—literally, "Today, I will open [or, inaugurate]/ my unprecedented [or, fantastic] festival [or, holiday]." Any combination of these possibilities in English would have sounded clumsy and silly; at least as importantly, none of the words in English capture the full semantic range of the Russian words, especially *nebyvalyi*, which dictionaries translate as "unprecedented" and "fantastic." "Fantastic" was out because it has come in modern English to mean something excellent and admirable. What was needed was a word which would express the idea of a revolutionary rupture in history, and an element of the improbable. We finally landed on "monstrous," which derives from the Latin *monstra*—nature- and history-rending portents, of the kind Tremens himself embodies. Likewise, "festival" and "holiday" both carry excessively positive and pleasurable connotations which do not do justice to *prazdnik* in this context. "Carnival," we felt, with its hints of flesh and anarchy, would complement the animal idea of the "monstrous" while contrasting with its implication of the unprecedented; just as, in the Russian, there is a paradox latent in the idea of a *prazdnik*, usually an annual festival, being *nebyvalyi*—unprecedented. We therefore arrived at our solution: "Today I shall unleash my monstrous carnival" (II.54).

A smaller example comes from the final scene of the play, in which Morn says that the crowd does "not know that the poor Eastern bride/is barely alive beneath her tasselled weight" (V.ii.128–29), where "tasselled weight" stands for *tiazhest'iu kosmatoi*, which would more literally be translated as "shaggy weight." Not only would "shaggy" have sounded comical, it would have made an obscure passage still more unclear: Morn here is looking for a female parallel to the image, in his previous speech, of a knight who seems glorious to the crowd but is hot and sweaty inside his armour (as Morn is dying within the prison of his fairy tale). The "Eastern bride" looks beautiful to the crowd but is suffocating within her heavy ornamental marriage robes. By "tasselled" we sought to translate *kosmatoi* in a way that would make this idea, if not obvious, at least accessible.

All our work was, however, doubled, if not tripled, by the demands of translating Nabokov's pentameter line. It was essential that *Morn*, with its high tragic ambition, remain a verse-play, but we soon decided against trying to reproduce Nabokov's own fairly strict iambic pentameter. It would have been impossible to do so without straying a long way from our primary goal of reproducing Nabokov's own nuances of sense. We opted instead for a loose five-stress line, evaluating the total rhythmic pattern of the line according to where the stresses seemed to us naturally to fall, in context. We have also tried if at all possible to pay respect to the integrity of each individual line and to avoid mean-

ingless line-endings and awkward enjambments. Therefore we
have not simply broken each line after ten or eleven syllables, and
have looked to create lines whose beginnings, endings, and pro-
gressive syntactic pattern are part of their poetic meaning.

We feel, nevertheless, that we have achieved a steady beat
throughout the play, and we have tried to make the rhythms rel-
evant to the sense and tenor of a particular speech. As is, indeed,
the established practice of English pentameter, the ear will, once
it is accustomed to the five-stress pattern, hear lines as five
stresses even where they are a syllable or two over or under
the established measure. Such "hypermetric" syllables are common in Shakespeare. In the case of split lines, we have allowed
ourselves greater liberty—as also with lines ending with an ellip-
sis (three dots), where the idea is that the line should seem to trail
off, so that there is a good reason for a stress to go missing. Some
characters' speeches, especially those of Dandilio and Tremens,
the play's two most grandiloquent orators, seemed naturally to
unfold into many-syllabled lines which verge on the hexameter—
appropriately, perhaps, in a play which gestures towards a lost
grandeur. Ganus thinks of the vanished King, saying that

> . . . His footsteps
> linger in the palace, like the step of a hexameter
> dwindling in one's memory . . .
> (III.ii.116–18)

Contrastingly, when Morn is reduced by his cowardice to the
lowly state of a bourgeois "mister," he muses that

> . . . I, I am Mister Morn—
> that is all; an empty space, an unstressed
> syllable in a poem without rhyme.
> (IV.177–79)

Such a slackening of rhythmic pressure characterizes the speeches of characters when they drop out of the high heroic mode; and we have attempted to capture this Shakespearean contrast of prosody and prose.

Lastly, a word on the edition we have translated. *Morn* survives in a typewritten copy and in a handwritten fair copy; neither is entirely complete, with a few passages missing in Act V. These texts were edited together by Serena Vitale and Ellendea Proffer for the 1997 *Zvezda* edition, and re-edited by Andrei Babikov for the 2008 Azbuka edition. It is this latter edition on which our translation is based.

—THOMAS KARSHAN, 2012

DRAMATIS PERSONAE

Main Characters

TREMENS

ELLA

GANUS

KLIAN

FOREIGNER

MIDIA

DANDILIO

MISTER MORN

EDMIN

Other Characters

SERVANTS

GUESTS (including FIRST GUEST, SECOND GUEST, LADY, GREY-HAIRED GUEST, SECOND VISITOR, THIRD VISITOR)

OLD MAN

FOUR REBELS

CAPTAIN and FOUR SOLDIERS

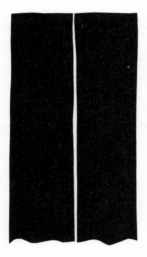

Act I.

Scene I

A room. The curtains are drawn. A fire blazes. TREMENS *sleeps in an arm-chair by the fire, wrapped up in a spotted blanket. He awakens heavily.*

TREMENS:
Dream, fever, dream; the soundless changing
of two sentinels standing at the gates
of my powerless life . . .
                              On the walls
the floral patterns form mocking faces;
the burning hearth hisses at me, not with fire   5
but with a serpent chill . . . O heart, O heart,
blaze up! Begone, fever, you snake! . . . Helpless
am I . . . But, O my heart, how I would like
to lend my trembling sickness to this fair
and careless city, so that the Royal Square   10
should sweat and blaze, as does my brow;
so that the barefoot streets should grow cold,
so that the whistling wind should shudder
the tall houses, the gardens, the statues
at the crossroads, the embankments, the ships   15
on the convulsing waters! . . .
    [*calls out*]
                              Ella! . . . Ella! . . .
    [ELLA *enters, elegantly coiffed but in a dressing gown.*]

TREMENS:

Give me some port and that glass phial,
the one on the right, with the green tag . . .
So, you are going dancing?

ELLA [*uncorks the decanter*]:

Yes.

TREMENS:

20   Will your Klian be there?

ELLA:

He will.

TREMENS:

Is it love?

ELLA [*sits down on the arm of the chair*]:

I don't know . . . It's all so strange . . .
It's not at all as it is in songs . . . Last night
I dreamt that I was a new white bridge,
made out of pine, I think, and covered in tears
25   of resin, thrown lightly over an abyss . . . And so
I waited. Alas, there were no timid footsteps—
the bridge yearned to yield sweetly, to crunch
in torment beneath the thunder of blind hooves . . .
I waited—and then, suddenly, I saw:
30   towards me, towards me, blazing, wailing,
whirled forth the form of a Minotaur,
with the broad chest and face of Klian!
Blissfully I surrendered—and awoke . . .

TREMENS:

I understand, Ella . . . Well, this pleases me—
35   it is my blood which has cried out in you,
my greedy blood . . .

ELLA [*preparing the medicine*]:

One drop . . . two drops . . . five,
six . . . seven . . . Enough?

6

TREMENS:

                    Yes. Get dressed,
go . . . it's late . . . Wait—stoke the fire . . .

ELLA:

Coals, coals, you blushing hearts . . . Fain burn!
  [*looks at herself in the mirror*]
How is my hair? I'll wear a gold gauze dress.   40
I am going . . .
  [*On her way out, she stops.*]
           . . . Oh, Klian brought me
his poems the other day; he sings them
so amusingly, flaring his nostrils slightly,
closing his eyes—like this, look—his palm
stroking the air as if it were a little   45
dog . . .
  [*Exits, laughing.*]

TREMENS:

        My greedy blood . . . And yet her mother
was so trusting and so tender; yes,
tender and cleaving, like pollen, drifting
through the air, onto my chest . . . Off with you,
you sunny piece of fluff! . . . Thank you, Death,   50
that you took this tenderness away from me:
free am I, free and reckless . . . Henceforth,
my servant Death, shall we oft agree . . . O,
I will send you out into this very night,
into those blazing windows above dark mounds   55
of snow; into those houses where life
twirls and dances . . . But I must wait . . .
It is not time yet . . . I must wait.
  [*Falls asleep. There is a knock at the door.*]

TREMENS [*shaking off sleep*]:

                  Come in! . . .

SERVANT:

There is, my lord, a man out there—a dark,
60   bedraggled man—he wants to see you . . .

TREMENS:

His name?

SERVANT:

He won't say.

TREMENS:

Let him in.

[SERVANT *exits. A* MAN *enters through the open door and stops
on the threshold.*]

TREMENS:

What do you want?

MAN [*slowly grinning*]:

. . . And still
the same spotted blanket on his shoulders . . .

TREMENS [*looks closer at him*]:

Forgive me . . . my eyes are bleary . . . but,
I do recognize, I recognize . . . Yes,
65   for certain . . . Is it you,—you? Ganus?

GANUS:

You weren't expecting me? My friend, my leader,
my Tremens, you weren't expecting me? . . .

TREMENS:

Four years, Ganus! . . .

GANUS:

Four years? Not years,
but stony boulders! Rocks, hard labour,
70   loneliness—and then—an indescribable
escape! . . . Tell me, how is my wife, Midia?

TREMENS:

She lives, she lives . . . Yes, I recognize you,
friend—the same Ganus, quick as fire,

8

the same passion in your speech and movements . . .
So you fled? And . . . what of the others?   75

GANUS:

I escaped—they still languish . . . You know,
I came to you, like the wind—straight away,
I've not yet been home . . . So you say, Midia . . .

TREMENS:

Listen, Ganus, I need to explain to you . . .
It is strange that the main rebel leader . . . No, no,   80
don't interrupt me! In truth, is it not strange
that I am free, when I know that my friends
suffer in black exile? I live just as before:
rumour does not name me; I'm still the same
twisted and secret leader . . . But believe me,   85
I did everything to burn in hell with you—
when they seized you all, I, incorruptible,
wrote a denunciation against Tremens . . .
Two days went by, on the third day I received
an answer. What was it? Well, listen: it was,   90
I remember, a dull and windy evening. I was
too lazy to put on the lights. It was growing
dark. I sat here and shook with fever,
rippling like a reflection in an ice-hole.
Ella had not yet returned from school. Suddenly—   95
a knock, and a man enters; his face obscured
in shadow, his voice muffled, as though it too
were tinged with darkness. Ganus, you are
not listening! . . .

GANUS:

                My friend, my dear friend,
you can tell me this later. I'm agitated,   100
I cannot follow. I want to forget, forget
all this—the smoke of revolutionary

conversation, the backstreets in the night . . .
Advise me, what shall I do: go to Midia now,
105   or wait? Oh, don't be angry! Don't! . . .
Please, go on . . .

TREMENS:

               Understand, Ganus, I must
explain! There are more important things
than earthly love . . .

GANUS:

                   . . . And so, this stranger . . .
tell me . . .

TREMENS:

            . . . was very strange. Quietly
110   he approached me: "The King has read your letter
and thanks you for it," he said, taking off
his glove, and a smile, it seemed, slipped across
his hazy face. "Yes . . ." the messenger
continued, theatrically slapping his glove,
115   "you are a clever conspirator, while the King
punishes only the foolish; from this follows
a conclusion, a challenge: walk free, magnet,
and gather up, magnet, the scattered needles,
the revolutionary souls, and when you gather them,
120   we'll sweep them up, and start again; so walk free,
shine on, attract . . ." Ganus, you are not listening . . .

GANUS:

On the contrary, my friend, on the contrary . . .
What happened next?

TREMENS:

               Nothing. He left,
calmly bowing . . . For a long time after, I stared
125   at the door. Since then, I rage in passionate
idleness . . . Since then I wait; I stubbornly await

a blunder from the strained powers that be,
so I can make a move . . . Four years I wait.
I dream enormous dreams . . . Listen, the time
is near! Listen, you living piece of steel,   130
will you be drawn to me again? . . .

GANUS:

                              I don't know . . .

I don't think so . . . You see, I . . . But Tremens,
you haven't told me about my Midia!
What does she do?

TREMENS:

                  Her? She strays.

GANUS:

How dare you, Tremens! I must confess   135
I am unused to your blaspheming words—
and I will not tolerate . . .

    [ELLA *has appeared, unnoticed, in the doorway.*]

TREMENS:

                     . . . in other times

you would have laughed . . . My right-hand man—
hard, clear, and free—has become tender,
like an ageing maid . . .   140

GANUS:

                Tremens, forgive me,

if I misunderstood your joke, but you
do not know, you do not know . . . I have
suffered greatly . . . The wind in the reeds
whispered to me of adultery. I prayed. I bribed
my creeping doubts with forced memories,   145
with the most winged, the most sacred ones,
which lose their colour as they fly into words,
and now, suddenly . . .

ELLA [*approaching*]:

Of course he was joking!

TREMENS:

Eavesdropping, eh?

ELLA:

No. I've long known—

150   you love equivocating little words,
riddles, that's all . . .

TREMENS [*to* GANUS]:

Do you recognize my daughter?

GANUS:

What, surely it can't be—Ella? That girl
who always lay spread out with a book, here
on this fur, while we reduced worlds to ashes? . . .

ELLA:

155   And you would blaze louder than the rest,
and smoke so much, sometimes, it seemed there were
not people but ghosts dancing in the grey-blue
waves . . . But how did you return?

GANUS:

I stunned
two sentries with a log and wandered lost

160   for half a year . . . And now, having finally
arrived, the fugitive dares not enter
his own home . . .

ELLA:

I go there often.

GANUS:

How nice . . .

ELLA:

Yes, I am very friendly with your wife.
Many a time in your dark drawing room

have we spoken of your bitter fate. In truth,   165
sometimes it was hard for me: for no one
knows that my father . . .

GANUS:

                     I understand . . .

ELLA:

                              Often,
in soundless splendour, she cried, as you know
Midia cries—silently and without blinking . . .
In the summer, we strolled in the city outskirts,   170
where you had strolled with her . . . Recently,
she told your fortune by looking at the moon
through a glass of wine . . . I'll tell you more:
this very evening I'm going to a party
at her house—there will be dancing, poets . . .   175
   [*points to* TREMENS]
Look, he has dozed off . . .

GANUS:

                   A party—
but without me . . .

ELLA:

               Without you?

GANUS:

                       I am
an outlaw: if they catch me, I'm done for . . .
Listen, I'll write a note—you can give it
to her, and I'll wait downstairs for an answer . . .   180

ELLA [*twirling around*]:
I've got it! I've got it! How splendid!
You see, I study at a theatre school,
I have paints and pomades here in seven
different colours . . . I'll smear your face in such

185   a way that God himself, on Judgement Day,
won't recognize you! Well, do you want to?

GANUS:

Yes . . . It's just that . . .

ELLA:

I'll simply say
that you're an actor, an acquaintance of mine,
and haven't taken off your make-up—
190   because it was so good . . . Perfect! It's not
up for discussion! Sit down here, closer
to the light. That's good. You shall be Othello—
the curly-haired, old, dark-skinned Moor.
I'll also give you my father's frock-coat
195   and black gloves . . .

GANUS:

How amusing: Othello
in a frock-coat! . . .

ELLA:

Sit still.

TREMENS [*grimacing, he wakes up*]:

Oh . . . I think
I fell asleep . . . Have you both lost your minds?

ELLA:

He cannot see his wife otherwise.
There will be guests there after all.

TREMENS:

Strange:
200   I dreamt that the King was being strangled
by a colossal negro . . .

ELLA:

I think our chance
remarks seeped into your dream, got mixed up
with your thoughts . . .

TREMENS:

Ganus, what do you suppose,
will it be long? . . . will it be long? . . .

GANUS:

What? . . .

ELLA:

Don't move your lips, talk of the King can   205
wait a little . . .

TREMENS:

The King, the King, the King!
Everything is full of him: the people's souls,
the air, and it is said that in the clouds
at sunrise, it is his coat-of-arms that shines,
and not the dawn. Meanwhile, no one knows   210
what he looks like. On coins he wears a mask.
They say, he walks amongst the crowds, sharp-sighted
and unrecognized, throughout the city,
in the market places.

ELLA:

I've seen him ride
to the senate, accompanied by horsemen.   215
The carriage gleams all over in blue lacquer.
On the door there is a crown, and in
the window the blind is lowered . . .

TREMENS:

. . . and, I think,
inside there's no one. Our King walks
on foot . . . And the blue lustre and the black steeds   220
are for show. He is a fraud, our King!
He should be . . .

GANUS:

Stop, Ella, you have
put paint in my eye . . . May I speak . . .

ELLA:

                                        Yes,
you may. I will look for a wig . . .

GANUS:

                              Tell me, Tremens,
225 I don't understand: what do you want?
     While wandering through the country I have
     noticed that in four years of radiant peace—
     after wars and revolutions—the country
     has grown wonderfully strong. And the King
230 alone achieved all this. What then do you want?
     New upheavals? But why? The power of the King
     is living and harmonious, it moves me now
     like music . . . I too find it strange, but I
     have understood that to rebel is criminal.

TREMENS [*rising slowly*]:

235 What did you say? Did I mishear? Ganus,
     you . . . repent, regret, and practically
     give thanks for your punishment!

GANUS:

                                        No.
     For the sorrows of my heart, for the tears
     of my Midia, I will never forgive the King.
240 But, consider: while we were declaiming
     grand words—on the oppressed, on poverty
     and the suffering of the people—the King
     himself was already acting in our stead . . .

TREMENS [*walks heavily around the room, drumming his fingers on
        the furniture as he passes*]:

     Hang on, hang on! Did you really think
245 that I worked with such determination
     for the good of an imaginary "people"?
     So that every manure-filled soul, some

drunken goldsmith or another, some gnarled
stable-boy could polish his dainty nails
up to a mirror sheen, and bend his little   250
finger back in affectation, when shaking
off his snot? No, you were mistaken! . . .

ELLA:

Move your head to the right a little . . . I'll pull
the astrakhan fur on for you . . .

                    Papa,
sit down, I beg you . . . You are dizzying me   255
with your movements.

TREMENS:

                    You were mistaken!
Revolts there may have been, Ganus . . . Time and again,
in city squares across the ages, have gathered
low-browed criminality, mediocrity,
and baseness . . . Their words I was repeating,   260
but I meant something more—and I had thought
that through those blunt words you felt my true fire,
and that your fire answered mine. But now,
your flame has tapered, it has turned to passion
for a woman . . . I feel great pity for you.   265

GANUS:

But what is it you want? Ella, don't get
in the way while I'm talking . . .

TREMENS:

                   Did you see,
one windy night, by moonlight, the shadows
of ruins? That is the ultimate beauty—
and towards it I lead the world.   270

ELLA:

                  Don't protest . . .
Sit still! . . . Press your lips together. A little

touch of arrogance . . . There. Some carmine
inside the nostrils—no, don't sneeze! Passion—
in the nostrils. Now yours are like those
275   of Arabian horses. There we go.
Please be quiet. After all, my father
is absolutely right.

TREMENS:

                You say:
the King is a great sorcerer. Agreed.
The sun has swollen the taut granaries,
280   the wonders of science are accessible to all,
labour is lightened by the play of hidden forces,
and the air is clean in the warbling workshops—
with all this I agree. But why do we
always want to grow, to climb uphill
285   from one to a thousand, when the downward path—
from one to zero—is faster and sweeter? Life
itself is the example—it rushes headlong
into ash, it destroys everything in its way:
first it gnaws through the umbilical cord,
290   then tears up plants and birds into shreds,
and our heart beats inside us like a greedy hoof,
till it smashes through our chest . . . And the poet,
who breaks up his thoughts into sounds? Or
the maiden, who prays for the blow of a man's love?
295   Everything, Ganus, is destruction. And
the faster it is, the sweeter, the sweeter . . .

ELLA:

                  Now
for the frock-coat, the gloves—and you're ready!
Really, Othello, I am pleased with you . . .
   [*declaims*]
"But yet I fear you; for you are fatal then

when your eyes roll so: why should I fear I know not,   300
since guiltiness I know not; but yet I feel fear . . ."
Oh, your boots are shabby—well, never mind . . .
GANUS:

Thank you, Desdemona . . .
   [*looking at himself in the mirror*]
                         Well, look at me!
It's been a while, it's been a while . . . Midia . . .
a masquerade . . . Lights, perfume . . . quick, quick!   305
Hurry, Ella!
ELLA:

           We're going, we're going . . .
TREMENS:

                           So,
you've decided to betray me, my friend?
GANUS:

Don't, Tremens! We'll talk some other time . . .
It's hard for me to argue now . . . Perhaps
you are right. Farewell, dear friend . . . You   310
understand . . .
ELLA:

           I won't be late . . .
TREMENS:

                     Go, go.
Klian has long been cursing you, himself
and everything else. Ganus, don't forget . . .
GANUS:

Hurry up, hurry up, Ella . . .
   [*They leave together.*]
TREMENS:

               So, you
and I are left alone, my serpent chill?   315
They're gone—my fugitive slave and poor

twirling Ella . . . Yes, seized and exhausted
by the simplest passion, Ganus seems to have
forgotten his true calling . . . But somehow
320   I sense that hidden within him is that spark,
that scarlet comma of contamination,
which will spread the wondrous cold and fire
of tormenting illness across my country:
deathly revolts; hollow destruction;
325   bliss; emptiness; non-existence.

CURTAIN

Scene II

A party at MIDIA's *house. The drawing room: to the left the entrance to the salon; to the right [at the back] a lighted niche by a tall window.* [MIDIA *with*] *several* GUESTS [*including* KLIAN, DANDILIO, *and the* FOREIGNER].

FIRST GUEST:
Morn says—though he himself is not a poet—
"It should be thus: in the flicker of daily life,
unexpectedly, in the chance combination
of light and shadow, you feel within yourself
the divine happiness of conception: 5
it grabs you and is gone; but the muse knows
that in a quiet hour, in the seclusion
of the night, the poem will begin to beat
and fly off the tongue, fiery and babbling . . ."

KLIAN:
I have never felt like that . . . I myself   10
create differently: with persistence, disgust,
tying a wet rag around my head . . . Perhaps
that's why I am the genius . . .
  [*Both of them pass on.*]

FOREIGNER:
                              Who is that—
the one that looks like a horse?

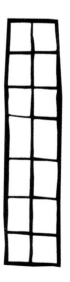

SECOND GUEST:

The poet Klian.

FOREIGNER:

15   Talented?

SECOND GUEST:

Shh . . . He's listening . . .

FOREIGNER:

And that one,
the silvery one, with the bright eyes—speaking,
at the doorway, to the mistress of the house?

SECOND GUEST:

You don't know? You sat beside him at dinner—
it is the carefree Dandilio, the grey-haired
20   lover of antiquity.

MIDIA [*to* DANDILIO]:

But why? It is
a sin: Morn, Morn and only Morn,
and the blood sings out . . .

DANDILIO:

There is no sin on earth.
Loves, sorrows—all are necessary, all
are beautiful . . . One must snatch the hours of fire,
25   the hours of love from life, as a slave grasps
at shells underwater—blindly, hungrily:
there is no time to prise them open, to choose
the sick one, with its precious tumour . . . They
shimmer, suddenly turn up, so grab at them
30   in handfuls, whatever's there, however you can—
and at that very moment when your heart
is bursting, you push off with your heel
convulsively, and, stumbling and panting,
empty out the treasure on the sunlit shore
35   at the feet of the Creator—he'll sort them out,

22

he knows . . . So let the broken shells be empty,
for the whole sea hums with mother of pearl.
And he who seeks only pearls, setting aside
shell after shell, that man shall come to
the Creator, to the Master, with empty hands—   40
and he will find that he is deaf and dumb
in heaven . . .

FOREIGNER [*approaching*]:

              I often heard your voice
in my childhood dreams . . .

DANDILIO:

                    Really, I never
can remember who has dreamt me. But
your smile I do remember. I meant to ask you,   45
courteous traveller, where have you come from?

FOREIGNER:

I have come from the Twentieth Century, from
a northern country, called . . .

    [*Whispers.*]

MIDIA:

                 Which one is it?
I don't know that one . . .

DANDILIO:

               How can you say that!
Don't you remember, from children's fairy tales?   50
Visions . . . bombs . . . churches . . . golden princes . . .
revolutionaries in raincoats . . . blizzards . . .

MIDIA:

But I thought it didn't exist?

FOREIGNER:

                  Perhaps. I
entered a dream, but are you sure that I
have left that dream? . . . So be it, I'll believe   55

in your city. Tomorrow I shall call it
a dream . . .

MIDIA:

Our city is beautiful . . .

[*She moves away.*]

FOREIGNER:

I find
in it a ghostly resemblance to the distant
city of my birth—that likeness which exists
60   between truth and high fantasy . . .

SECOND GUEST:

It is,
believe me, the most beautiful of all cities.

[SERVANTS *serve coffee and wine.*]

FOREIGNER [*with a cup of coffee in his hand*]:
I am struck by its spaciousness, by its clean,
extraordinary air: in it music sounds
differently; houses, bridges, and stone arches,
65   all the architectural outlines in it,
are boundless, light, like the passage
from the happiest sigh to sublime silence . . .
I am also struck by the ever-cheerful gait
of passers-by; the absence of cripples;
70   the melodious sound of footsteps and of hooves;
the flight of sledges across white squares . . . And
they say the King alone has done all this . . .

SECOND GUEST:

Yes, the King alone. Gone are the times
of hardship, never to return. Our King—
75   a masked giant, in a fiery cloak—
took the throne by force, and that very year
the last wave of revolts died down.
A conspiracy was uncovered: its members

were swept aside—and, by the way,
Midia's husband too, although one shouldn't   80
mention it—and sent to distant mines,
from whence the law will never call them back;
I say the members, for the main rebel,
their nameless leader, was never found . . .
Since then, the country has been at peace.   85
Ugliness, boredom, blood—all have evaporated.
The pure sciences reach for lofty heights,
but, recognizing beauty in the past,
the King has protected poetry, the agitation
of bygone ages—horses, and sails, and live   90
ancient music—although alongside these,
there wander through the air transparent,
electrical birds . . .

DANDILIO:

              In bygone days
flying machines were otherwise constructed:
sometimes they would flap upwards,   95
to the thunder of the glinting propeller,
to the explosion of petrol, emitting a smell
of tea into the empty sky . . . Forgive me,
but where is our interlocutor? . . .

SECOND GUEST:

                    I didn't
notice how he disappeared . . .   100

MIDIA [*approaching*]:

               And now
the dances will begin . . .

    [*Enter* ELLA, *with* GANUS *behind.*]

MIDIA:

             And here's Ella! . . .

FIRST GUEST [*to the* SECOND GUEST]:

   Who is that blackamoor? What a scarecrow!

SECOND GUEST:

   And to think he's wearing a frock-coat! . . .

MIDIA:

   You are so luminous . . . so ethereal . . .

105   How is your father?

ELLA:

                    Still the same: fever.

   Here, do you remember, I told you?—

   our tragic hero . . . I begged him to keep

   his make-up on . . . It is Othello . . .

MIDIA:

                         Very good!

   Klian, come here . . . tell the violinists

110   to begin . . .

      [*The* GUESTS *move through into the salon.*]

MIDIA:

            Why does Morn not come?

   I do not understand . . . Dandilio!

DANDILIO:

   But one must love even anticipation.

   Anticipation is a flight into the dark.

   Then all at once there's light, a fall into

115   the happy light, but then the flight is over . . .

   Ah, music! Please, allow me to offer

   you my arm.

      [ELLA *and* KLIAN *walk past.*]

ELLA:

           Is something bothering you?

KLIAN:

   Who is your consort? Who is your black-faced

   consort?

ELLA:

    A harmless actor, Klian. Why,
are you jealous?   120

KLIAN:

          No. No. No.
I know that you are faithful to me, my bride . . .
O, God! To enter you, oh, to enter,
would be like entering a tight and searing
sheath, to peer into your blood, to break
through your bones, to learn, to grasp, to touch,   125
to press your being in between my palms! . . .
Listen, come to me! It is a long time
until spring, until our wedding day! . . .

ELLA:

Don't, Klian . . . you promised me . . .

KLIAN:

Oh, come to me! Let me break into you!   130
It is not I who beg, but my starved genius,
tormented by you, writhes in the ashes,
scrunching its wings, it begs . . . Oh, understand,
it is not I who beg, not I! See—
the muse wrings her hands . . . there is a wind   135
in the Olympian gardens . . . Pegasus's eyes
are filled with blood and dawn . . . Ella, will you come?

ELLA:

Don't ask, don't ask. It scares me, it delights me . . .
You know, I am only a white bridge,
I am but a flimsy bridge over the torrent . . .   140

KLIAN:

Tomorrow then—at ten sharp—your father
goes to bed early. At ten. Yes?
    [GUESTS *walk past.*]

FOREIGNER:

Who then
do you think is the happiest in this city?

DANDILIO [*taking snuff*]:

It's me, of course . . . I have deduced happiness,
145   determined it, like a scientific theorem . . .

FIRST GUEST:

I want to make a correction. In our city
each and every one will answer: "It's me,
of course!"

SECOND GUEST:

No. There is one unhappy man:
that dark conspirator, unknown to us,
150   the one who wasn't caught. Somewhere he lives,
even now, and knows that he is guilty . . .

LADY:

That poor negro there is also unhappy.
He wanted to astonish everyone
with his frightening appearance, but nobody
155   has taken notice of him. Awkward Othello
sits in the corner, drinking gloomily . . .

FIRST GUEST:

. . . and looks out from under his brow.

DANDILIO:

And what
does Midia think?

SECOND GUEST:

Look, our stranger
has disappeared again! It is as though,
160   passing between us, he slipped behind the curtain . . .

MIDIA:

I think, happiest of them all is the King . . .
Ah, Morn!

[MISTER MORN *enters, laughing, with* EDMIN *following.*]
MORN [*as he walks*]:
                Splendid, blissful people! . . .
VOICES:
    Morn! Morn!
MORN:
                Midia! Greetings, Midia,
radiant lady! Give me your hand, Klian,
you thunderous madman, you crimson soul!   165
Ah, Dandilio, you gay dandelion . . .
Music, music, I need heavenly music! . . .
VOICES:
    Morn is here, Morn!
MORN:
                    Splendid, blissful
people! What snow, Midia . . . what snow!
As cold as the kiss of a ghost, as hot as tears   170
on your eyelashes . . . Music! Music! And who
is this? An ambassador from the East?
MIDIA:
    An actor, a friend of Ella's.
FIRST GUEST:
                    Before you came,
we were trying to decide who is the happiest
in our city; we thought—the King; but then   175
you entered: first place is yours, I think . . .
MORN:
    What is happiness? The flutter of celestial wings.
    What is happiness? A snowflake on one's lip . . .
    What is happiness? . . .
MIDIA [*quietly*]:
                    Listen, why did you
come so late? The guests will be leaving soon: 180

it looks like my belovèd deliberately
arrived for their departure . . .
MORN [*quietly*]:

My joy, forgive me:
work . . . I have been very busy . . .
VOICES:

Dancing!
Dancing!
MORN:

Ella, may I have this dance . . .
[*The* GUESTS *move into the salon. Only* DANDILIO *and*
GANUS *remain.*]
DANDILIO:

185   I see Othello is missing Desdemona.
Oh, the demon is in that name . . .
GANUS [*glancing in the direction of* MORN]:

What a
passionate gentleman . . .
DANDILIO:

What can one do, Ganus . . .
GANUS:

What did you say?
DANDILIO:

I said, has it been long
since you left Venice?
GANUS:

Leave me, I beg you . . .
[DANDILIO *moves into the salon.* GANUS *is left hunched at a
table.*]
ELLA [*enters briskly*]:

190   Is there anyone here?

GANUS:

                    Ella, this is

hard on me . . .

ELLA:

               What is wrong, my dear?

GANUS:

There is something I don't understand.
This suffocating make-up feels like
it's straining my heart . . .

ELLA:

                   My poor Moor . . .

GANUS:

Before, you said . . . I felt so happy . . .   195
You were telling the truth, weren't you?

ELLA:

                       Come on,

smile . . . Listen, the violin bows are
sparkling from the hall!

GANUS:

              Will it end soon?

This heavy, mottled dream . . .

ELLA:

                Yes, soon, soon . . .

    [GANUS *moves into the salon.*]

ELLA [*alone*]:

How strange . . . my heart suddenly sang out: 200
I would give my whole life for this man
to be happy . . . a kind of light breeze
has passed by, and now I feel capable
of the most humble feat. My poor Moor!
I'm such a fool, why did I bring him with me?   205
I never noticed before—only just now,

in feeling jealousy on his behalf,
did I at long last see that some secret
reverberating sound connects Midia
210 to swift Morn . . . All this is strange . . .
DANDILIO [*comes out, looking for someone*]:

Did
you see? Did that Foreigner come past here?
ELLA:

I didn't see him . . .
DANDILIO:

What a curious fellow!
He slipped away like a shadow . . . We were
just having a conversation with him . . .
[ELLA *and* DANDILIO *pass on.*]
EDMIN [*leads* MIDIA *to a chair*]:
215 You do not dance tonight, Midia?
MIDIA:

While you,
as always, are mysteriously silent—
perhaps you would like to tell me what
Morn does all day?
EDMIN:

What does it matter?
Whether he's a businessman, a scholar,
220 an artist, a warrior, or just an impassioned man—
isn't it all the same to you?
MIDIA:

And what
is it you do yourself? Stop it—stop shrugging
your shoulders! Conversation with you
is such a bore, Edmin . . .
EDMIN:

I know . . .

MIDIA:

Tell me, when Morn is here, you guard, alone   225
beneath the window, and after leave with him.
Friendship is friendship, but this . . .

EDMIN:

I like it this way.

MIDIA:

Is there not a woman—unknown to us—
with whom you would more pleasantly spend
the nights, while Morn is here, than with the spectre   230
of someone else's happiness? . . . How foolish—
you've grown pale . . .

[MORN *enters, wiping his brow.*]

MORN:

What is happiness?
Klian ran past me and, like the wind,
took Ella from me . . .

[*to* EDMIN]

Friend, brighten up!
Your face is painfully contorted, as though   235
you were about to sneeze . . . Go dance . . .

[EDMIN *exits.*]

. . . Oh, my Midia, how you do resemble
happiness! No, do not move, do not spoil
your splendour . . . I am cold from happiness.
We are on the crest of a wave of music . . . Wait,   240
don't speak. This very moment is the peak
of two eternities . . .

MIDIA:

A mere two moons
have rolled by since that vivid day, when
mysterious Edmin brought you to me. That day
you conquered me with the piercing glance   245

33

of your deep eyes. In them, an intense force
sparkles around the pupils with a yellow light . . .
Sometimes it seems to me that, walking
down the street, you could, with the even breath
250   of your eyes alone, inspire in passers-by
whatever you wanted: happiness, wisdom,
the heat of passion . . . I'll put it this way—
but don't laugh: my soul has fixed itself
to your eyes, as when in childhood
255   one's tongue sticks to cloudy metal if,
for a lark, you lick it in the flaring frost . . .
Now tell me, what do you do all day?

MORN:

And your eyes—no, show me—are
slightly slanted, satin-like . . . Oh, my dear . . .
260   May I kiss the rays of your collarbone?

MIDIA:

Wait, be careful—that black tragedian
is watching us . . . soon the guests will leave . . .
Be patient!

MORN [*laughing*]:

          Well, that should not be hard:
A whole night will make me tire of you
265   yet . . .

MIDIA:

        Don't joke like that, I don't like it . . .
[*The music dies down. The* GUESTS *exit the salon.*]

DANDILIO [*to the* FOREIGNER]:

Wherever did you disappear to?

FOREIGNER:

I had woken up. The wind roused me.
It rattled the window frame. I barely
fell back asleep . . .

DANDILIO:
People here will find
that hard to believe. 270
MORN:
Ah, Dandilio . . .
I haven't had a chance to talk with you . . .
What new things have you collected? What
rusty screws, what bracelets of pearl?
DANDILIO:
Things
are bad. Recently I found a fiery parrot—
huge and sleepy, with a crimson feather 275
in his tail—I found him in a little shop,
where he sits remembering the tunnel
of a smoking tropical river . . . I would have
bought him but I have a cat—these two
divine, mysterious creatures could not live 280
together . . . Each day I go and admire him:
he is a sacred parrot, he does not speak.
FIRST GUEST [*to the* SECOND GUEST]:
Time to go home. Take a look at Midia,
I think her smile is a suppressed yawn.
SECOND GUEST:
No, wait, they're bringing more wine. Let's drink. 285
FIRST GUEST:
But it's getting rather dull . . .
MORN [*opening a bottle*]:
Here! Fly,
you cosmic cork, into the stuccoed heavens!
Burst forth, foam, like chaos, gushing, welling . . .
whoa . . . between the fingers of the Creator.
GUESTS:
To the King! To the King! 290

DANDILIO:

How about you, Morn?
Will you not drink?

MORN:

Certainly not. One gives
one's life to the King, but drink—why
on earth drink?

FOREIGNER:

To this happy kingdom.

KLIAN:

To the Milky Way!

DANDILIO:

This wine will make
295   the stars flow in our heads . . .

ELLA:

Down in one,
to the fiery parrot!

KLIAN:

Ella, to our "tomorrow"!

MORN:

To the mistress of the house!

GANUS:

I want to ask . . .
It is unclear to me . . . Can we not toast
the previous master of the house?

MIDIA [*dropping her glass*]:

There.
300   All over my dress.
[*Pause.*]

FIRST GUEST:

Put salt on it.

DANDILIO:

There is
a saying: with the tears of happiness, any stain
immediately disappears . . .

MIDIA [*to* ELLA, *quietly*]:

Listen, your actor
is drunk, I think . . .
[*Wipes her dress.*]

MORN:

I read in a rare treatise—
here, Dandilio, you are a man of books—
that, while creating the world, God made a joke   305
at just the wrong moment . . .

DANDILIO:

In that same book,
I remember, it is also said that a guest
is as necessary to a house as air,
but if the breath drawn in is not released—
you will turn blue and die. So, Midia . . .   310

MIDIA:

What! So early?

DANDILIO:

It's time, it's time. My cat
is waiting . . .

MIDIA:

Do come again . . .

FIRST GUEST:

It's also time
for me, lovely Midia.

MIDIA:

That's terrible!
You should stay . . .

ELLA [*to* GANUS, *quietly*]:

                        I beg you, please

315   also leave . . . You can visit her tomorrow

morning . . . She's tired.

GANUS [*quietly*]:

                           I . . . don't understand?

ELLA [*quietly*]:

Where is the joy in a reunion when one

is tired?

GANUS [*quietly*]:

                    No, I will stay . . .

[*Moves off into semi-darkness by the round table. Meanwhile
the* GUESTS *have been saying goodbye.*]

FOREIGNER [*to* MIDIA]:

                           I won't

forget my stay in your bewitching city:

320   the closer a fairy tale is to reality,

the more magical it is. But I fear something . . .

Trouble is ripening here unseen . . . In

the splendour, in the mirrors, I sense it . . .

KLIAN:

Don't listen to him, Midia! He is only

325   here by chance. Quite the magician! I happen

to know he's just a merchant's errand boy . . .

he carries specimens of foreign goods around . . .

Is that not so? He's slipped away!

MIDIA:

                        How funny

he is . . .

ELLA:

        Farewell, Midia . . .

MIDIA:

                     Why so cold?

ELLA:

Not at all . . . I'm a little tired . . .   330

EDMIN:

                  I too

shall go . . . Goodnight.

MIDIA:

                    Foolish man!

    [*She laughs.*]

SECOND GUEST:

                      Farewell.

If a guest really is like a breath of air,

then I leave here like a short, sad sigh . . .

    [*Everyone leaves except* MORN *and* GANUS.]

MIDIA [*stands in the doorway*]:

Till next week.

    [*returns to the centre of the drawing room*]

               Ah, finally!

MORN:

              Shh . . .

We're not alone.   335

    [*Points to* GANUS *sitting inconspicuously.*]

MIDIA [to GANUS]:

          I say, you are far kinder

than my other guests, you've stayed . . .

    [*Sits down beside him.*]

                    Tell me,

where have you acted? Your terrifying make-up

is excellent . . . Have you known Ella long?

A child . . . like wind . . . like a glimmer of water . . .

Klian is in love with her, the one with   340

the Adam's apple and the horse's mane—

a bad poet . . . No, really, it is frightening,

you are truly, truly an Arab . . . Morn, stop
whistling through your teeth . . .

MORN [*at the other end of the room*]:

> You have

345   a nice clock here . . .

MIDIA:

> Yes, it is very old . . .

In its depths there plays a crystal brook . . .

MORN:

It's good . . . It's a little slow, don't you think? . . .

MIDIA:

Yes, I do . . .

> [*to* GANUS]

> And you . . . Is your home

far from here?

GANUS:

> It's close. Nearby.

MORN [*by the window, yawning*]:

> What stars . . .

MIDIA [*nervously*]:

350   It must be slippery out in the street . . .
The snow has been spiralling since morning . . .
I was at the ice-rink today . . . Morn flutters
like a bird on ice . . . why is the chandelier
lit for no reason . . .

> [*quietly to* MORN *as she passes by*]

> Look—he's drunk . . .

MORN [*softly*]:

355   Yes, he was plied by Ella . . .

> [*approaches* GANUS]

> It's very late!

Time to go home. It's time, Othello!
Do you hear?

GANUS [*heavily*]:

> Well, what can I say . . .

I dare not keep you . . . go . . .

MIDIA:

> Morn . . . I'm scared . . .

His voice is thick, as though he's strangling someone! . . .

GANUS [*gets up and approaches*]:

> Enough . . . I will reveal my voice . . . enough!　　　360

I do not have the strength to wait any longer.

Off with my glove!

> [*to* MIDIA]

> > Are you familiar

with these fingers?

MIDIA:

> Oh! Morn, you must leave.

GANUS [*passionately*]:

> Greetings! Are you not pleased? For it is I—

your husband! Risen from the dead!　　　365

MORN [*utterly calmly*]:

> Risen indeed.

GANUS:

> You are still here?

MIDIA:

> > Don't!

I beg you both! . . .

GANUS:

> Damned fop! . . .

MORN:

> > The hot whistle

of your black glove pleases me. I

answer it with mine . . .

MIDIA:

> Ah! . . .

[*She runs to the back of the stage, towards the niche, and opens the window in jerks.* MORN *and* GANUS *fight with their fists.*]

MORN:

The table,

370   you'll knock over the table! . . . What a windmill! . . .
Don't swing your arms around so much! The table . . .
the vase! . . . I knew that would happen! . . . Ha-ha!
Stop tickling! Ha-ha! . . .

MIDIA [*shouts out of the window*]:

Edmin! Edmin! Edmin! . . .

MORN:

Ha-ha! The make-up's running! . . . There, tear up

375   the carpet! . . . Go on! Don't wheeze, don't yelp! . . .
Fight more cleanly! Here comes a comma
and a full stop!

[GANUS *collapses in a corner.*]

MORN:

Blockhead . . . He's undone my tie.

EDMIN [*rushes in, pistol in hand*]:

What happened?

MORN:

A mere two blows: the first
is called "a hook," the second "a left jab."

380   And, by the way, this gentleman here is—
Midia's husband . . .

EDMIN:

Is he dead?

MORN:

Not likely . . .
Watch, he'll come to now. Ah, welcome
back! This is my second at your service . . .

[*He notices that* MIDIA *is lying unconscious at the back of the stage, near the window.*]

O, God! My poor love! . . . Edmin . . . wait . . .
Yes, call someone . . . Oh, my poor love . . .   385
You shouldn't have, you shouldn't have . . . really . . .
We were just playing . . .

    [*Two* MAIDS *rush in: they and* MORN *attend to* MIDIA *at the*
    back of the stage.]

GANUS [*gets up heavily*]:

                    I . . . accept . . . the challenge.
Horrible . . . give me a handkerchief . . . or something . . .
How horrible . . .

    [*wipes his face*]

                  Ten paces apart and the first
shot is mine . . . by right: I am the wronged party . . .   390

EDMIN [*looks around frantically*]:

Listen . . . wait . . . you may find this strange . . .
But I must . . . ask you . . . to decline the duel . . .

GANUS:

I don't understand? . . .

EDMIN:

                  If you wish, I will take
his place . . . face your bullet . . . I am ready . . .
Right now, if you like . . .   395

GANUS:

                  Evidently I am
losing my mind.

EDMIN [*quietly and briskly*]:

                Well then, I'll break my vow! . . .
I will reveal it to you . . . duty requires me . . .
But you must swear to me, on love, disdain,
or on your hatred, on what you will, that you
will never speak of this terrible secret . . .   400

GANUS:

. . . I'm sorry, but what is all this about?

43

EDMIN:

    Here, I'll reveal it to you, he—this man—

    he is . . . oh, I can't!

GANUS:

                Hurry up!

EDMIN:

    Oh, come what may! He is . . .

    [*Whispers in his ear.*]

GANUS:

                    That's a lie!

    [EDMIN *whispers.*]

405   No, no . . . It cannot be! O, God . . .

    what should I do? . . .

EDMIN:

              You must decline!

    There is no other way . . . Decline! . . .

MIDIA [*to* MORN *at the back of the stage*]:

                    My joy,

    don't leave . . .

MORN:

          Wait . . . let me just . . .

GANUS [*firmly*]:

                     No!

EDMIN:

    Why did I break my . . .

MORN [*approaching*]:

             So, have you decided?

GANUS:

410   Yes, we have decided. But I'm not much

    of a murderer: we shall fight *à la courte paille*.

MORN:

    Excellent . . . A solution has been found. We

    shall agree the details tomorrow. Goodnight.

May I add that duels are not to be
discussed with ladies. Midia could not bear it.   415
Keep silent to the end. Let's go, Edmin.
   [*to* MIDIA]
I'm leaving, Midia . . . Be calm . . .
MIDIA:

                           Wait . . . I'm frightened . . .
What was the outcome?
MORN:

                       Nothing. We made up.
MIDIA:
Listen, take me away from here! . . .
MORN:

                         Your eyes
are like swallows in autumn, when they cry out: 420
"Southwards . . ." Let me go . . .
MIDIA:

                          Wait, wait . . .
You're laughing through tears! . . .
MORN:

                      Through rainbows, Midia!
I am so happy that my happiness,
as it glimmers, overflows the brim.
Adieu—Edmin, let's go. Adieu. All's well . . .   425
    [MORN *and* EDMIN *leave. Pause.*]
GANUS [*slowly approaches* MIDIA]:
Midia, what is all this? Oh . . . say something—
my wife, my bliss, my madness—I am waiting . . .
Tell me all this is a joke, a motley, evil
masquerade, in which a gentleman in tails
strikes a painted Moor . . . do smile! For I   430
am laughing . . . I'm cheery . . .

MIDIA:

I don't know what

to say to you . . .

GANUS:

Just say one word; I will
believe anything . . . anything . . . Empty jealousy
intoxicated me—is that not so?—

435 like wine drunk in port after one's been
long tossed at sea. O, say something . . .

MIDIA:

Listen, I will explain . . . You left—that much
I remember. God saw how I grieved.
Your things spoke to me, they smelled of you . . .

440 I was unwell . . . But gradually my memory
of you lost its warmth . . . You grew cold
in me—you were still living and yet
already incorporeal. Then you became
transparent, a kind of familiar ghost;

445 and finally, faint and translucent, you left
my heart on tiptoe . . . I thought—forever . . .
I resigned myself. And then my heart
renewed itself and came alight. I wanted
so much to live, to breathe, to whirl about.

450 Oblivion granted me freedom . . . And now,
suddenly, you come back from the dead, now,
suddenly, you burst so violently into a life
that's foreign to you . . . I don't know what to say
to you . . . How do I talk to a ghost who has

455 come back to life? I just don't know . . .

GANUS:

The last

time I saw your face was through bars.
You lifted up your veil, to dab your nose—

with a crumpled handkerchief—like this,
like this . . .

MIDIA:

                Who is to blame? Why did you leave?
Why did you need to fight—against happiness,   460
against fire and truth, against the King? . . .

GANUS:

Ha-ha . . . The King . . . O, God . . . The King! . . .
This is madness . . . madness! . . .

MIDIA:

                    You frighten me—
don't laugh like that . . .

GANUS:

                 It's nothing. It has passed . . .
Three nights I have not slept . . . I'm rather tired.   465
All autumn-long I wandered lost. Understand,
Midia, that I fled: I could not stand
my punishment . . . I came to know the sleepless
sound of night pursuits. I starved.
I too cannot tell you . . .   470

MIDIA:

                . . . And all this
just to paint your face, and afterwards . . .

GANUS:

But I wanted to please you!

MIDIA:

                  . . . and afterwards
to be beaten and to roll around
like a drunken fool in the corner,
and to forgive the wrongdoer everything,   475
and to turn the insult into a joke,
to humiliate yourself in front of me . . .
Disgusting! Take this pillow, smother me!

For I love another! . . . Smother me! . . . No,
480 all he can do is cry . . . Enough . . . I'm tired . . .
Go . . .

GANUS:

Forgive me, Midia . . . I didn't know . . .
It is as though for four years I eavesdropped
at a door, entered it—and found no one.
I'll leave. Just let me see you . . . Once a week,
485 no more . . . I will live at Tremens's. Only
don't go away . . .

MIDIA:

Let go of my knees!
Leave . . . do not torture me . . . Enough—
I will go mad! . . .

GANUS:

Farewell . . . Don't be angry . . .
forgive me—for I did not know. Give me
490 your hand—no, just to say goodbye. I must
look funny—I've smudged my make-up . . . Well . . .
I'm leaving . . . Lie down . . . It's getting light . . .
[*Leaves.*]

MIDIA:

Fool!

CURTAIN

48

TREMENS's *room.* TREMENS *is in the same pose as in act I, scene i.*
GANUS *sits at the table, laying out playing cards.*

TREMENS:
  The bliss of emptiness . . . Non-existence . . .
  So shall I keep repeating to you, until
  with trembling hands you squeeze together
  your exploding head; until I deafen your soul
5 with the thunders of my devastating dream! . . .
  I am tormented by idleness, and yet I know
  that my stifled will is like the water, which,
  falling drop after drop upon the head
  of a condemned man, gives birth to madness,
10 gnawing his skull and eating through his reason;
  like water, which, seeping drop after drop
  through stone, into the fiery bowels of the earth,
  provokes the eruption of a volcano—
  the madness of the earth . . . Non-existence . . .
15 Though I have fallen in love with twilight,
  I must live on and suffer the stings of life,
  that I may give the people the joy of eternal
  death—yet my steadfast soul does not cry out,
  crucified though it be on the bone cross

of the human skeleton, on the black thunderous   20
Golgotha of existence . . . You are pale, Ganus . . .
Stop laying out those cards, stop ruffling your
wild hair and glancing at the face of the clock . . .
What's there to fear?

GANUS:

              Be quiet, I beg you! It's quarter to . . .
This is unbearable! The clock-hands move   25
like hunchbacks; like a widow and an orphan
behind a catafalque . . .

TREMENS:

             Ella! My medicine!

GANUS:

Tremens . . . No, don't let her come in!
O, God!

    [ELLA *enters lazily, dragging her shawl behind her.*]

ELLA:

        It's cold in here . . . I'm not sure
that clock is right . . .   30
    [*Looks at the wall-clock.*]

TREMENS:

            What's it to you?

ELLA:

                    Nothing.
Strange: the fire is lit, but it's cold . . .

TREMENS:

                 My cold,
Ella, it's my cold! I feel the chill of life,
but wait—soon I will let loose such fire . . .

GANUS:

This is unbearable! Ella, you're jangling
the glass bottles . . . for God's sake, don't . . .   35

What was I about to say? Oh, yes:
the other day you promised to give me
an envelope and a stamp . . .

TREMENS:

> . . . With a masked man . . .

ELLA:

I'll fetch them. It's cold here . . . Maybe I am
40   imagining it. I keep yawning all day . . .
>   [*Leaves.*]

GANUS:

What did you say?

TREMENS:

> I said that the stamp
depicts our noble . . .

GANUS:

> Tremens, Tremens, O,
if you only knew! Not that. Listen, I
deliberately asked Ella . . . You must send
45   her away, somewhere, for an hour . . . They are
coming now: we decided on ten o'clock,
you checked the cartel yourself . . . I beg you,
give her an errand . . .

TREMENS:

> On the contrary, Ganus.
Let her learn. Let her see fear and courage.
50   Death is a spectacle worthy of the gods.

GANUS:

You are a monster, Tremens! How can I,
under the gaze of her child-like eyes . . . O
Tremens, I beg you! . . .

TREMENS:

> Enough. It's part of my plan.
Today I shall unleash my monstrous carnival.

Your opponent—now what's his name? I have   55
forgotten . . .

GANUS:

        Tremens! My friend! Six minutes remain!
I implore you! They're coming now . . . It's Ella
I pity!

TREMENS:

      . . . your opponent is just some flitting,
flashy buffoon; but if he should draw death
from the fist by its little white ear, I would be   60
content: one less soul on this earth . . . Oh, how
I long to sleep . . .

GANUS:

       Five, five minutes left! . . .

TREMENS:

Yes: this is the hour I go to bed . . .

   [ELLA *returns.*]

ELLA:

Here, take them. I could barely find them . . .
My face drifts up out of the semi-darkness   65
to meet me, like a murky jellyfish, and
the mirror is like black water . . . And my hair
is tired and dishevelled . . . And I—a bride.
I—a bride . . . Ganus, are you happy for me? . . .

GANUS:

I don't know . . . Yes, of course I'm happy . . .   70

ELLA:

After all, he's a poet, he's a genius,
unlike you . . .

GANUS:

      Yes, Ella . . . Well, well . . .
soon the clock will strike . . . strike through my soul . . .
Oh, what does it matter! . . .

ELLA:

                              Can I ask you
75   something? You have told me nothing, Ganus—
      what happened there when we left? Ganus!
      Well, then—he's silent . . . Are you really angry
      with me? Truly, I did not know that our
      little masquerade would not come off . . .
80   How can I help? Perhaps there are some words—
      they flower in the shadows of high songs,—
      I'll find them. What a foolish, sulking man,
      he bites his lips, and doesn't want to know me . . .
      I will be understanding . . . Look at me . . .
85   It is sinful to be silent with me. What else
      is there for me to say?

GANUS:

                              What, Ella, what
      do you want from me? You want to talk?
      Oh, let's, let's talk! About anything you want!
      About unfaithful women, about poets,
90   about spirits, about the blind gut and its
      missing glasses, about fashion, about the planets—
      whisper, roar with laughter, chatter over
      one another, chatter ceaselessly! Well,
      what then? I'm having fun! . . . O, God! . . .

ELLA:

                                        Don't! . . .
95   You're hurting me . . . You cannot understand.
      Don't. Ah! It's striking ten . . .

GANUS:

                              Ella—look—
      I'll tell you . . . I must ask you to . . . Listen . . .

ELLA:

      What card is that? Even?

GANUS:

Yes, it's even—
what difference does it make . . . Listen . . .

ELLA:

An eight.

I've thought of a number. Klian will be waiting   100
at ten. When I go—it will all be over. The card
says—to stay . . .

GANUS:

No—go! Please, go!
It is meant to be! Believe me! I know—
love does not wait! . . .

ELLA:

Listless languor
and a slight chill . . . Is that really love?   105
In any case, I shall do as you tell me . . .

GANUS:

Go, quickly, quickly!—before he wakes up . . .

ELLA:

No, but why? He will allow me to go . . .
Father, wake up. I'm leaving.

TREMENS:

Oh . . . the pain . . .

Where are you going so late? No, stay,   110
I need you.

ELLA [*to* GANUS]:

Shall I stay?

GANUS [*quietly*]:

No, no, no . . .

I beg you, I beg you! . . .

ELLA:

You . . . You . . . are

pitiful.

[*She goes out, throwing on a fur wrap.*]

TREMENS:

    Ella! Wait! Damn her . . .

GANUS:

    She's gone, gone . . . The door downstairs crashed
115   like glassy thunder . . . I feel relieved now . . .

    [*Pause.*]

    It's after ten . . . I don't understand . . .

TREMENS:

    To be late is duelling etiquette. Or maybe
    he's lost his nerve.

GANUS:

                  There is another rule
    as well: not to insult someone else's
120   opponent . . .

TREMENS:

                  And I will tell you this: the soul
    must fear death as a maiden fears love. Ganus,
    what do you feel?

GANUS:

                 The fire and cold of revenge,
    and I stare steadily into the cat-like eyes
    of steely fear: the animal tamer knows
125   that he need only turn away—the beast
    will spring. But, fear apart, there is another
    feeling, gloomily watching over me . . .

TREMENS [*yawns*]:

    Damned drowsiness . . .

GANUS:

               This feeling is the worst
    of all . . . Here, Tremens, a business letter—
130   send it by post; here, a letter to my wife—

give it to her yourself . . . Oh, how it sticks
in the throat, oh, how it sticks! . . . Stay calm . . .

TREMENS:

                                  So.

Did you look at the stamp? I can always feel
that taut neck under my fingers . . . You must
help me, Ganus, if death spares you . . . Help me . . .   135
We'll find some savage mercenaries . . . We'll
penetrate the gloomy palace . . .

GANUS:

                             Don't
distract me with your mad drowsy muttering.
For me, Tremens, this is very hard . . .

TREMENS:

                            Sweet sleep . . .
Everlasting sleep . . . My lashes stick together.   140
Wake me . . .

GANUS:

                   He sleeps. He sleeps . . . fiery and blind!
Shall I reveal it to you, shall I? Oh, how
late they are! The anticipation will kill me . . .
O, God! Shall I reveal it? It's all so simple:
not a meeting, not a duel, but a trap . . .   145
one short gunshot . . . Tremens himself will do it,
not I, and he will say that I have placed
higher than honour the cold duty of a rebel,
and he'll give thanks to me . . . Away, away,
trembling temptation! There is but one reply,   150
but one reply to you,—the disdainful one—
it is ignoble. Ah, here—they come . . . Oh,
that carefree laugh behind the door . . . Tremens!
Wake up! It's time!

TREMENS:

What! Oh! They've come?

155   Who is that laughing there? A familiar lilt? . . .

[MORN *and* EDMIN *enter.*]

EDMIN:

Allow me to introduce Mister Morn.

TREMENS:

Delighted to be at your service. Have we met?

MORN [*laughs*]:

I don't recall.

TREMENS:

In my half-sleep it seemed . . .

But it doesn't matter . . . Where is the arbiter?

160   That sprightly old man—Ella's godfather—

what's his name . . . oh, my memory!

EDMIN:

Dandilio

will be here shortly. He doesn't know anything.

It's better that way.

TREMENS:

Yes, fate is blind. That's

an old joke. Sleep overcomes me. Forgive me,

165   I am unwell.

[*Two groups: to the right, by the fire,* TREMENS *and* GANUS; *to the left, on the darker side of the room,* MORN *and* EDMIN.]

GANUS:

Waiting . . . more waiting . . .

I'm getting weak, I cannot bear this . . .

TREMENS:

Oh,

Ganus, poor Ganus! You are the mirror

of suffering; oh, to breathe some warmth

into you to cloud the glass! Look, for instance:
a kind of warm shadow swathes your opponent.   170
He gazes at my paintings, whistles quietly . . .
I cannot see, but it seems his face is calm . . .

MORN [*to* EDMIN]:

Look: a green meadow, and there, beyond it,
a forest of firs in black oils, a pair
of clouds pierced by slanting golden light . . .   175
the time is nearly evening . . . and in the air,
perhaps, a church bell . . . the midges swarm . . .
Ah, to go there, to go into that picture,
into the reverie of its green, airy colours . . .

EDMIN:

Your calm is a pledge of immortality.   180
You are magnificent.

MORN:

             You know, it amuses me:
I have been here before. It amuses me,
I keep wanting to laugh . . . My unhappy
opponent dares not look me in the eye.
I repeat that you were wrong to tell him . . .   185

EDMIN:

But I wanted to save half the world! . . .

TREMENS [*from his chair*]:

Which is the picture you like? I can't see—
is it the birches over a backwater?

MORN:

             No,—
evening, a green meadow . . . Who painted it?

TREMENS:

He is dead. Only his cold bones remain.   190
Something is crucified on them—rags, a soul . . .

Oh, I really don't know why I keep
these paintings. Leave them, you mustn't
look at them!

GANUS:

Ah! A knock at the door! No,
195   it's someone with a tray. Tremens, Tremens,
do not laugh at me! . . .

TREMENS [*to the* SERVANT]:

Put it here.
Here, drink this, Ganus.

GANUS:

I don't want it.

TREMENS:

As you wish. My dear sirs, I pray do not
refuse.

MORN:

Thank you. But tell us, Tremens, when
200   was it that you stopped painting?

TREMENS:

When I became
a widower.

MORN:

And are you now not tempted
to put your thumb through the palette once more?

TREMENS:

Listen, we've gathered to decide on death,—
a question of high importance; this is no place
205   for small talk. Let us talk of death. You laugh?
So much the better; but let us talk of death.
What is the ecstasy of death? It is a pain,
like lightning. The soul is like a tooth, God
wrenches out the soul—crunch!—and it is over . . .
210   What comes next? Unthinkable nausea and then—

the void, spirals of madness—and the feeling of being
a swirling spermatozoid—and then darkness,
darkness—the velvety abyss of the grave,
and in that abyss . . .

EDMIN:

       Enough! This is worse
than talking about a bad painting! Here.   215
Finally.

  [*The* SERVANT *shows in* DANDILIO.]

DANDILIO:

     Good evening! Ooph, how hot it is
in here! It's been a while, Tremens, since
we've seen each other—you live like a hermit.
I was astounded by your invitation:
but the wise man, they say, invites the moth.   220
For Ella—here—a box of glossy sugar plums—
she loves them. Greetings, Morn! Edmin,
you must be sleeping badly. You are as pale
as a lily of the valley . . . Ah—can it really
be Ganus? We once were well acquainted. It   225
is a secret, is it not, that you have returned
to us? When last night you and I . . . how did
I know? Well, by the brand, by the blue number—
here—above your wrist: you wrung your hands
and the number was revealed. I noticed it,   230
and, as I recall, I said that in Desdemona . . .

TREMENS:

Here, have some wine, biscuits. Soon Ella
will be back . . . You see, I live quietly,
but happily. Pour some for me. By the way,
there's been a disagreement here: these   235
gentlemen here want to decide which
of them shall pay for a dinner . . . in honour

of some fashionable dancer. If you could
just . . .

DANDILIO:

Of course! I'll pay with pleasure!

TREMENS:

No, no,

240   not that . . . clasp the handkerchief and let out
two ends—one with a knot.

MORN:

Which can't be seen,
of course. Really, he's a child—one must explain
everything! Do you recall, you carefree dandelion,
how one night I planted you atop a street lamp:

245   the light shone through your grey tufts,
and you were trying to pull a shaggy top hat
over the moon and smacked your lips so happily . . .

DANDILIO:

And after that, the top hat smelled of milk.
You prankster, I forgive you!

GANUS:

Hurry . . . We asked you . . .

250   This must be resolved . . .

DANDILIO:

Come, come, my friend—
patience . . . Here is my handkerchief. Not
a handkerchief but a multicoloured flag.
Forgive me. I'll turn my back to you . . . Ready!

TREMENS:

He who pulls out the knot shall pay. Ganus,

255   pull.

GANUS:

No knot!

MORN:

        You are lucky, as always . . .

GANUS:

I can't . . . what have I done! I shouldn't have . . .

TREMENS:

He clutches his head, mutters—but it's not you—
he's the one who's lost.

DANDILIO:

          Forgive me, what's this . . .

I have made a mistake . . . There is no knot,
I didn't tie one, look—what a miracle!   260

EDMIN:

Fate, fate, fate decided thus! Listen
to fate. That's the outcome! I beseech
you—beseech you—to be reconciled!
All is well!

DANDILIO [*taking snuff*]:

        And I shall pay for the dinner . . .

TREMENS:

The art connoisseur looks worried . . . Enough   265
jesting with fate: give me that handkerchief!

DANDILIO:

What do you mean—give it to you? I need it—
I sneeze,—it's covered in tobacco, it's damp;
and what is more—I have a cold.

TREMENS:

        We'll make it

simpler, then! Here, with cards . . .   270

GANUS [*mumbling*]:

        I can't.

TREMENS:

Quick, which suit?

MORN:

Well, I love the colour
red—life, and roses, and sunrises . . .

TREMENS:

Now
I shall show the card! Ganus, stop!
What a fool he is—he's gone and fainted!

DANDILIO:

275   Hold him—oh, he's heavy! Hold him, Tremens,—
my bones are made of glass. Ah, there—
he's come to.

GANUS:

God, forgive me.

DANDILIO:

Let's go, let's go . . .
lie down.

[*He leads* GANUS *to the bedroom.*]

MORN:

He could not bear the repetition
of his good fortune. So. The eight of clubs.
280   Very good.

[*to* EDMIN]

You've grown pale, friend? Why?
To set in contrast still more sharply
the black silhouette of my fate? Sometimes
despair is the finest of all artists . . . I am
ready. Where is the pistol?

TREMENS:

Not here, though,
285   please. I don't like mess in my house.

MORN:

Yes,
you are right. Sleep soundly, worthy Tremens.

My house is taller. The shot will resound
more sonorously in it, and tomorrow
will come a dawn in which I have no part.
Let's go, Edmin. I shall spend the night   290
at Caesar's.

    [MORN *and* EDMIN *exit, the former supporting the latter.*]
TREMENS [*alone*]:

                Thank you . . . My chill has been
replaced by a flowing warmth . . . How pleasing is
that grin anticipating death and the mortal
glimmer in his eyes! He keeps his spirits up,
he plays . . . I have no interest in the actor   295
himself, yet—strange—it still seems to me
that this is not the first time I have heard
his voice: as when one remembers the tune
but not the words; perhaps there are none:
only a movement of thought—and the tune   300
itself melts away . . . I am content with today's
motley scenes, with these images of the unknown.
Yes! I am pleased—and feel in my veins
a living languor, a warmth, a thaw . . . Now!
Climb out of my sleeve, thou five of diamonds!   305
I don't know how it happened, but, inspired
by a momentary pity, I substituted
the card I'd grabbed—the raspberry rhombuses—
with another, the one I showed. One—two!
The eight of clubs!—if you please!—and death   310
peered out of its funereal clover at Morn!
While the fools were talking of roses—a slip
of the palm, a sleight of hand—so swiftly
is fate made. But never shall my Ganus
know that I cheated, that it was to him,   315
fortunate man, that death fell . . .

[DANDILIO *returns from the bedroom.*]
DANDILIO:

They've left?
But they forgot to bid me farewell . . . This
snuffbox is an antique . . . For three centuries
tobacco wasn't taken—and now it's fashionable
320 again. Would you like some?
TREMENS:

What's wrong with Ganus?
A fit?
DANDILIO:

It's nothing. He's pressed to the bed, muttering
something and flinging out his hands, as though
to catch, by their coat-tails, invisible passers-by.
TREMENS:

Leave him,—it's good for him. He'll learn.
DANDILIO:

Yes,
325 all grain is grist for the mill of the soul, you're right . . .
TREMENS:

I meant something else. Ah, the steps
of my infatuated Ella! I know,
I know where she has been . . .

[ELLA *enters.*]
ELLA:

Dandilio!
DANDILIO:

What is it, my dear, what, my lightness? . . .
ELLA:

Only
330 splinters remain . . . splinters! He . . . Klian . . .
O, God . . . Don't touch me! Leave me . . . I am sticky . . .
I am drenched in cold pain. Lies! Lies!

Surely this cannot be what they call bliss.
It's death, not bliss! My soul has been brushed
by the coffin lid . . . pinched . . . it hurts . . .   335
TREMENS:
That is my blood. Let her cry.
DANDILIO:
There . . .

there . . . Let me brush away that lock . . .
You have pearls and roses on your cheeks,
a shimmer, your hair is dewy from the snow . . .
You're being silly. All is well. While playing,   340
a child scratches itself—and cries. Life,
its skirts flying up and rustling, will run
through all the rooms, like a young mother,
fall down upon her knees before the child,
and, laughing, will kiss the scratch away . . .   345

CURTAIN

ACT III.

Scene I

A huge study. A starry night can be seen through the tall windows, but the stage is in darkness. Two figures [MORN and EDMIN] enter cautiously.

MORN:
> And so, it's over. I'll spend the night at Caesar's! . . .
> And so, it's over, dear friend . . . For the last time,
> like two regicides, have we stolen after midnight
> by the secret passages, into my palace . . . Light
> a candle. The wax will drip—stand it straighter.   5
> One more . . . there. Better than a sober lamp!
> Now listen. I foresaw the possibility
> of death. Here, in this table, in its oak
> and malachite depths, sleep my papers—
> contracts, plans, the drafts of laws . . . and   10
> dried flowers . . . I hand the keys to you.
> I also hand over this will, in which it states
> that in a fit of sweet and blinding visions,
> I decided to yield to death. Let my crown,
> —like a taut ball kicked aside,—be caught,   15
> and clasped in the arms of my young nephew;
> let the grey-haired owls—the senators, in whose
> charge he is—noiselessly govern my country,

whilst on the throne sits but a little boy,
20 dangling his legs . . . But the people must not
know. Let my carriage, with its blue lacquer
and coat-of-arms gleaming, rush as before
along the square and over the bridge. I will
become a ghost. And when my heir grows up,
25 I want him to reveal how it was I died:
he will begin the fairy tale with a fairy tale.
My mantle, embroidered with flames, may fit
him perfectly . . . You, Edmin, my confidant,
my subtlest counsellor, soften the edges of power
30 with your light subtlety, encircle its movements
with your serenity . . . You understand?

EDMIN:

I'll do it all . . .

MORN:

One thing more: today,
in a meditative hour, I wrote a childish,
but to me necessary, edict—that anyone
35 who is successful in escaping exile
will be pardoned for his courage . . .

EDMIN:

I'll do it all.
And if you would only hint, with one
movement of your eyelids, that I should
accompany you into unknown eternity . . .

MORN:

40 . . . Light these candles too. Let the mirrors
be filled with visions, with winds . . . I shall return
shortly. I am going to the chamber where
for four years now my fiery crown has burned
and breathed in its velvet nest; let it squeeze

my head with its diamond pain, let it roll   45
off my head when I fall backwards . . .
EDMIN:

                             My sovereign,

my precious friend . . .
MORN:

                      . . . Not a shot, no, not
a shot! A musical explosion! As though
for a moment a door opens to the heavens . . .
While here—how the strings will prolong   50
the sound! What a fairy tale shall I leave
to the people! . . . You know, in the dark I hit
my knee upon the chair. It hurts.
    [*Leaves.*]
EDMIN [*alone*]:
O, I am like wax! . . . The chronicles will not
forget this weakness of mine . . . I am to blame . . .   55
Why do I not rush to save him? . . . Rise up,
rise up, my soul! No, heavy drowsiness . . .
I could with prayers, persuasions—I know
that such exist—stop him . . . why not, then?
As a man in his dreams cannot move his arm—   60
so I have not the strength even to contemplate
what is about to happen . . . This is—retribution! . . .
When once, in childhood, I was forbidden to go
to the apiary, I for a moment held
in my mind the thought of my mother's death, and how,   65
unsupervised, I would eat the clear honey,—
though I loved my mother to tears, with trembling
heart . . . This is—retribution. Now, once more
I'm stuck to the sweet honeycombs. One thing
alone I see, one thing burns in the twilight: 70

come morning I will bear news of his infidelity!
Like some criminal, befogged by wine, I'll enter,
I'll speak, Midia will cry . . . and not hearing
my own words, and trembling, and with tender,
75 hypocritical consolation, touching her
imperceptibly, I will lie to her, so as
to take the place of someone else. Yes,
lie, tell her—about what?—the supposed
unfaithfulness of him, before whom we two—
80 are dust! If he had lived I would have kept
silent till the end . . . But now my god will leave . . .
I'll be alone, weak and greedy . . . Death is better!
O, if only he would order me to die!
Burn, weak-willed wax . . . Breathe, mirrors,
85 with a funereal flame . . .

> [*He lights the candles. There are many of them.* MORN
> *re-enters.*]

MORN:

                            Here's the crown.
My crown. Droplets of waterfalls on spikes . . .
Edmin, it's time. Tomorrow you shall call
the senate together . . . announce . . . secretly . . .
Farewell then . . . it's time . . . Before my eyes
90 pillars of fire surge past . . . Yes, listen—
one last thing . . . go to Midia, tell her
that Morn is the King . . . no, not the King,
not that. You'll say: Morn is dead . . . wait . . .
no . . . say: he's left . . . no, I don't know!
95 It's better you make something up,—but
it shouldn't be about the King . . . And say it
very quietly, and very softly, as is your way.
Why are you crying like that? Don't . . . Get up
off your knees, get up . . . your shoulder blades

72

are shaking like a woman's . . . Don't cry, dear friend . . .   100
Go . . . into the other room: when you hear
the gunshot—come back in . . . Enough, I die
merrily . . . Farewell . . . Go . . . wait! Do you
remember how once we stole in darkness
from the palace, and a sentry fired at me,   105
and shot through my collar? . . . How we laughed
then . . . Edmin? He's gone . . . I am alone,
and all around are flaming candles, mirrors,
and a frosty night . . . Brightness and terror . . .
I am alone with my conscience. So, here's   110
the pistol . . . an antique . . . six rounds . . . I need
but one . . . Hey, who is there above the rooftops?
You, God? Forgive me, then, what people
will not forgive! What's better—standing or sitting?
Sitting is better. Quick. Just don't think! . . .   115
Snap—the cartridge, in! The muzzle to the chest.
Below the rib. Here's the heart. Like so.
Now the safety catch . . . goosebumps on my chest.
The muzzle's cold, like the lacquer tube
applied by a doctor: he breathes in, he listens . . .   120
and his bald pate and the tube rise up
in rhythm with my chest . . .
                              No, wait!
That is not how people shoot themselves . . .
This needs to be thought through . . . One. Two.
Three. Four. Five. Six. Six steps from the chair   125
to the window. The snow shines. How starry
is the sky! God, give me strength,
give me strength, I beg you—give me strength . . .
There sleeps my city, all in hoar-frost,
all in a blue shroud. O, my dear! . . . Farewell,   130
forgive me . . . I ruled for four years . . . created

73

an age of happiness, an age of harmony . . . God,
give me strength . . . Playfully, lightly I ruled;
I appeared in a black mask in the ringing hall,
135   before my cold, decrepit senators . . . masterfully
I revived them—and left again, laughing . . .
laughing . . . And sometimes, in patched-up clothes,
I sat in a tavern and grunted with the ruddy
drunken coachmen; a dog would wag its tail
140   under the table, and a girl would tug me
by the sleeve, though I looked like a pauper . . .
Four years passed, and now, in the radiant noon
of my life, I must abandon my kingdom, must
jump from the throne to death—O, God,—all
145   because I kissed a shallow woman and struck
a foolish adversary! I could have had him . . .
O conscience, conscience—the cold angel
at the back of thought: thought turns—there's
no one there; but behind, it rises up again.
150   Enough! I must, must die! O, if only
it could not be so, not so, but in sight
of the world, in the hot storm of battle,
to the thunder of hooves, atop a sweaty steed,
so as to greet death with an immortal cry
155   and gallop headlong through the sky into
heaven's yard, where the splash of water
can be heard, and a seraph scrubs the horse
of St. George! Yes, death would be rapture then! . . .
But here I am—alone . . . only candle flame—
160   a thousand-eyed spy—watches from under
the suspicious mirrors . . . But I must die!
There is no glory—there is eternity
and man . . . What's this crown for? It digs
into my temples, damned thing! Off with it!

Like so . . . like so . . . roll across the dark carpet,   165
like a wheel of fire . . . Now quickly! Don't think!
Plunge reason in icy water! One movement:
press the curved trigger . . . One movement . . .
How many times have I pressed door handles,
the buttons of doorbells . . . And now . . . And now . . .   170
I don't know how! My finger on the trigger
is weaker than a worm . . . What's a kingdom to me?
What's valour? To live, only to live . . . O, God!
Edmin!
    [*approaches the door; calls out like a child*]
        Edmin!
    [EDMIN *enters.* MORN *stands with his back to him.*]
            I can't . . .
    [*Pause.*]
                        Why do you
stand there, why do you look at me? Or,   175
perhaps, you think that I'm a . . . Listen, here,
I'll explain . . . Edmin, you understand . . . I love her . . .
I love Midia! My kingdom and my soul
I am prepared to yield, if only not
to part from her! My friend, listen, do not   180
blame me . . . do not blame me . . .
EDMIN:
                        My sovereign, I'm happy . . .
You are my hero . . . I'm not even worthy . . .
MORN:
                                Really?
Really? . . . Well then . . . I'm pleased . . . Earthly love
is higher, stronger, than heavenly valour . . . Though you,
Edmin, don't love . . . you cannot understand   185
that a man is capable of burning worlds
for a woman . . . So then—it is decided.

I'll flee from here . . . there is no other way.
For in truth—I ruled without a care.
190 Such carelessness is power. That has gone.
Oh, how can I rule, when the Devil himself
has melted the crown on my poor head?
I'll disappear . . . You understand, I'll disappear,
I'll quietly live out the rest of my strange life
195 to the secret tune of my royal memories.
Midia will be with me . . . Why do you keep silent?
Am I not right? Midia will die without me . . .
You know that.

EDMIN:

My sovereign, I ask but
one thing: an agonizing request, a crime
200 against my native land . . . though it be!
I beseech you: take me with you . . .

MORN:

O, how you love me, how you love, dear friend! . . .
I have not the power to refuse you . . . I am
a criminal myself. Listen, do you remember
205 how I came to power? I came out in a mask
and mantle on the golden balcony,—it was
windy, it smelled, for some reason, of the sea,
and the mantle kept slipping off, and from behind
you righted it . . . But, why do I . . . Quickly,
210 time is running on . . . there is this will here . . .
How to change it? . . . What shall we do? How
to act? In it, I write that . . . Burn it! Burn it!
Thankfully the candles are lit. Quick! Meanwhile,
I'll compose a different one . . . But how? My mind
215 is empty. I move my quill as if on water . . .
Edmin, I don't know. Advise me—we must hurry,
to finish by sunrise . . . What's wrong?

EDMIN:

                                       Footsteps . . . They're
coming here . . . Along the gallery . . .

MORN:

                                           Quick!
Put out the lights! We'll have to go through
the window—oh, hurry! I can't meet with anyone . . .   220
Come what may . . . What shall I take? Yes,
the pistol . . . put them out . . . put them out . . . the
   papers . . .
the diamonds . . . right. Fling it open! Hurry . . .
My trenchcoat has caught—wait. Ready! Jump! . . .
   [*They leave. Darkness onstage. An* OLD MAN *in livery, stoop-*
   ing, comes in with a candle in his hand.]

OLD MAN:

Looks like somebody's been messing about in here . . .   225
A burning smell. Table's out of place . . . Hark you now—
Look where they've thrown the crown. Ptfu . . . Ptfu . . .
   Shine . . .
I'll rub you . . . And there—that casement's wide open.
That won't do . . . Let's have a listen at the door.
   [*Sleepily he crosses the stage and listens.*]
The rascal's asleep . . . the master sleeps. For   230
it's gone four, I dare say . . . O, Lord Jesus!
Oh, how my bones ache, how they ache! Cook
shoved some ointment at me,—says, try it,
rub some on . . . Try arguing . . . That's all I need . . .
Old age isn't some ugly mug daubed on   235
a fence, you can't just paint over it . . .
   [*And, muttering, he exits.*]

CURTAIN

Scene II

The same stage set as in the previous scene: the King's study. Only now the carpet is torn in places and one of the mirrors is broken. Four of the REBELS, *seated. Early morning. In the window the sun is visible, and there is a bright thaw.*

FIRST REBEL:

    The firing at the western gate still opens
    wide its swift embraces, so as to catch—
    now a soul, now a melody, now the ringing
    of glass . . . smoke rises from the houses still,
5   from the hunched ruins of the senate, the museum
    of coins, the museum of banners, the museum
    of old statues . . . We are tired . . . All night long—
    work, tumult . . . It must be past seven already . . .
    What a morning! The senate blazed, like a torch . . .
10   We're tired, confused . . . Where's Tremens rushing us?

SECOND REBEL:

    The draughty skeleton has clothed itself in flesh
    and fire. It's come to life. It rubs its hands.
    The mob gleefully tears open the cellars, marvels
    at the fires . . . I don't know, don't know, brothers,
15   what he's planning . . .

THIRD REBEL:

Not so, not so, did we
once think to make our homeland happy . . . I regret
the sleepless nights of exile . . .

FIRST REBEL:

He is mad!
He ordered that the flying machines be burned
so as to entertain the drunkards! But some
nameless heroes came along, and grabbed   20
the controls just in time . . .

FOURTH REBEL:

This order here,
that I am copying out, is terrifying
in its tigerish playfulness . . .

SECOND REBEL:

Quiet . . .
Here comes his son-in-law . . .
        [KLIAN *enters hurriedly.*]

KLIAN:

Splendid news!
In the suburbs the merry crowd's blown up   25
a school; satchels and rulers are scattered across
the square; about three hundred little mites
perished. Tremens is very pleased.

THIRD REBEL:

He's . . .
pleased! Brothers, brothers, do you hear?
He's pleased! . . .   30

KLIAN:

Well, then, I'll inform the leader
that my news did not much please you . . .
Everything, I shall report everything!

SECOND REBEL:

> We say
> that Tremens is wiser than us: he knows his goal.
> As it says in your last ode, he is a genius.

KLIAN:

35 Yes. He is worthy of entering the thunders
of my melodies. Nonetheless . . . the sun . . .
dazzles my eyes.
> [*Looks out of the window.*]
> Ah—there's that traitor,
Ganus! There, between the soldiers, standing
at the barriers: they're laughing. They have
40 let him through. There he goes across
the melting snow.

FIRST REBEL [*watching*]:

> How pale he is!
Our former friend is unrecognizable!
Everything about him—his gaze, his pursed lips—
reminds one of the saints in stained glass . . .
45 They say his wife has fled . . .

SECOND REBEL:

> Was there a lover?

FIRST REBEL:

I don't think so.

FOURTH REBEL:

> Rumour has it that one day
he came to his wife, and on the table there was
a note, that come what may she had decided
to go, alone, back to her family . . . Klian,
50 what's so funny about that?

KLIAN:

> I shall report
everything! Here you are, spinning rumours,

like old women, whilst Tremens thinks that
you are working . . . There are fires out there,
they need to be fanned, whilst you . . . I'll report
everything, everything . . .   55

    [GANUS *stops in the doorway.*]

                    Ah! Noble Ganus . . .
Most welcome Ganus . . . We were waiting for you . . .
We're glad to see you . . . Please . . .

FIRST REBEL:

                    Our Ganus . . .

SECOND REBEL:

Greetings, Ganus . . .

THIRD REBEL:

              Do you not recognize us?
Your friends? Four years . . . together . . . in exile . . .

GANUS:

Away, you hirelings of a liar! . . . Where's Tremens?   60
He summoned me.

KLIAN:

            He's interrogating.
He'll be here soon . . .

GANUS:

             Well, I don't need him.
He invited me himself, and if . . . he's not here . . .

KLIAN:

Wait, I'll call him . . .

    [*Goes towards the door.*]

FIRST REBEL:

            And we will go too . . .
Is that not so, brothers? Why stay here . . .   65

SECOND REBEL:

                    Yes,
so much to do . . .

THIRD REBEL:

Klian, we're coming with you!

[*quietly*]

Brothers, I'm scared . . .

FOURTH REBEL:

I'll finish copying later . . .

I'll go . . .

THIRD REBEL:

Brother, brother, what are we doing . . .

[KLIAN *and the* REBELS *leave.* GANUS *is alone.*]

GANUS [*looks around in all directions*]:

. . . A hero lived here . . .

[*Pause.*]

TREMENS [*enters*]:

Thank you for coming,

70   my Ganus! I know that you've been clouded
by the sorrows of life. You've scarcely noticed
that for a month—a month today exactly—
I have ruled over an intoxicated country.
I called for you, so you could tell me directly,

75   could explain . . . but first let a fortunate man
talk of his happiness! You know yourself—
better than anyone, Ganus—that I waited
for my day, in a delirium, in a chill . . .
My day has come—unexpectedly, like love!

80   Rumour spread like a flame that the country
had no king . . . When and how he disappeared,
who strangled him, on what night, and how long
a dead man ruled the land, nobody now knows.
But the people do not forgive deceit:

85   the burial vaults, the senate, were filled
with angry trampling. How splendidly,
how austerely, the old men died, and how

he screamed—O, sweeter than an ardent violin—
the little boy, their ward. The people took revenge
for the deception,—I seized the opportunity   90
to blaze up, and realized that I had waited so long
in vain: there was no king at all—only
a legend, potent and magical! Awakening,
the mob stormed in here, and nothing but echoes
resounded through the dead palace! . . .   95
GANUS:

                                    You called

for me.
TREMENS:

        You are right, let's turn to business:
in you, Ganus, I divined a kindred fire;
to you alone I entrusted my thoughts.
But you were tormented by a woman;
now she is gone; I'm going to ask you,   100
Ganus, for the last time: will you help me?
GANUS:

You summoned me in vain . . .
TREMENS:

                            Think it over,
don't rush, I will give you a little time . . .
    [*Hurriedly* KLIAN *enters.*]
KLIAN:

My leader, those people, the ones who recently
were singing in the streets, are being tortured . . .   105
There is no one to interrogate them . . .
Your assistants—how can I put it—are feeling
nauseous . . .
TREMENS:

              All right, I'm coming, I'm coming . . . You,
my Klian, are a fine fellow! . . . I've long known . . .

110   By the way, one of these days I will
        surprise you: I'll order that you be hanged.

KLIAN:

        Tremens . . . My leader . . .

TREMENS:

                        As for you, Ganus,
        think it over, I ask you, think it over . . .

            [TREMENS *and* KLIAN *leave.*]

GANUS [*alone*]:

        A single thought torments me: here lived a hero . . .
115   these mirrors here are sacred: they looked on him . . .
        He sat here, in this mighty chair. His footsteps
        linger in the palace, like the step of a hexameter
        dwindling in one's memory . . . Where did he die?
        Where did his shot ring out? Who heard it?
120   Perhaps it was out there, outside the city,
        in a mournful oak forest, in the snows of night . . .
        and his pale friend buried the hot corpse
        in a drift of snow . . . Sin, inconceivable sin,
        how can I expiate you? All of my blood
125   is grateful for the death of my rival and yet
        all of my soul curses the death of the King . . .
        We are duplicitous, we're blind—and it is hard
        to live, trusting only in life: earthly life
        is a murky translation from the divine original;
130   the general thought is clear but the primordial
        music is missing in its words . . . What are passions?
        Mistakes in the translation. What is love?
        A rhyme lost in transmission to our discordant
        language . . . It's time for me to take up the original! . . .
135   My dictionary? One simple little book with a cross
        on its cover . . . I'll seek out the stony arches, there,

where the respite of prayer and the full breath
of the soul will teach me the pronunciation
of life . . .
       There in the doorway, Ella has stopped,
and does not see me, deep in thought,   140
fingering the fringes of her sluggish shawl . . . What
can I say to her? She needs warmth . . . Dear one . . .
She doesn't see me . . .

ELLA [*aside*]:
              How amusing! . . . I opened
and read someone else's letter . . . Handwriting
like the wind, and the smell of the south . . . I   145
resealed it, just as father once showed me
in jest . . . Morn and Midia are together!
How can I give it to him? He thinks that she
is living in that old-fashioned backwater
that she comes from . . . How to give it to him? . . .   150

GANUS [*approaching*]:
You're up early. Me too . . . We seldom meet
now, Ella: another festivity coincided
with your wedding . . .

ELLA:
           Morning—an azure
miracle—and not a morning . . . it trickles . . . whispers . . .
Has Klian gone?   155

GANUS:
         He's gone . . . Tell me, Ella,
are you happy?

ELLA:
       . What is happiness? The flutter
of wings, or perhaps a snowflake on one's lip—
that is happiness . . . Who said that? I don't recall . . .

No, Ganus, I was wrong, you know . . . But
160   how bright it is today, it's practically spring!
Everything trickles . . .

GANUS:

Ella, Ella, did you ever
think that the daughter of a powerless rebel
would live in a palace?

ELLA:

Oh, Ganus, I miss
our little old rooms, our peace, the fireplace,
165   the paintings . . . Listen: lately I've come to realize
that my father is mad! We have fallen out
with one another; now we're not speaking . . .
I believed in it at first . . . What for! Rebellion
for the sake of rebellion is both boring
170   and horrifying—like night-time embraces
without love . . .

GANUS:

Yes, Ella, you have truly
understood . . .

ELLA:

The other day all the squares
gazed at the sky . . . Laughter, screams, howls
of fury . . . Saving themselves from the flames,
175   the flyers soared up from all directions, came
together like crystal swallows, and quietly
the shimmering flock slipped away. One
fell behind and froze for a moment above
the tower, as though he had left his nest there,
180   and then unwillingly caught up his sorrowful
companions,—and all of them melted away
into a crystal dust in the sky . . . I realized,
when they had disappeared, when in my eyes

swam blinding circles—from the sun—
I suddenly realized . . . that I love you . . .   185
[*Pause.* ELLA *looks out of the window.*]
GANUS:

I have
remembered! . . . Ella, Ella . . . How frightening! . . .
ELLA:

No, no, no—keep silent, dear. I look
at you, I look into the palace garden,
I look into myself, and now I know
that all is one: my love and the raw sun,   190
your pale face and the bright trickling icicles
beneath the roof, the amber spot upon
the porous sugary snow mound, the raw sun
and my love, my love . . .
GANUS:

I've remembered:
it was ten o'clock, and you left, and I   195
could have stopped you . . . Yet another blind,
momentary sin . . .
ELLA:

I don't need anything
from you . . . Ganus, I will never tell you again.
And if I told you now, it was only because
the snow today is so translucent . . . Really,   200
all is well . . . Days follow days . . . And then
I will become a mother . . . other thoughts
unwillingly will occupy me. But now,
you are mine, like the sun! Days will flow
after days . . . What do you think—perhaps   205
one day . . . when your sorrow . . .
GANUS:

Don't ask me, Ella!

I don't want to even think of love!
I answer like a woman . . . Forgive me . . . But I
burn with something other, I'm filled with something
210   other . . . I dream only of the austere wings,
the straight brows of angels. For a while
I will go to them—away from life, away
from fires, away from greedy dreams . . . I know
a monastery entangled by cool wisteria.
215   There I will live; through iridescent glass
I'll look on God, listen as the bellows
of the organ breathe the world's soul
up to the triumphant heights, and think
about vain feats, about a hero who prays
220   in the murk of sleeping myrtles, amidst
the fire-flies of Gethsemane . . .

ELLA:

                            Oh, Ganus . . .
I forgot . . . here, a letter came yesterday . . .
addressed to my father, with a note saying
it's for you . . .

GANUS:

                            A letter? For me? Show me . . .
225   Ah! I knew it! Don't . . .

ELLA:

                            So, can I
tear it up?

GANUS:

                Of course.

ELLA:

                            Give it to me . . .

GANUS:

                                    Wait . . .
I don't know . . . that smell . . . that handwriting,

which flies headlong into my memory,
into my soul . . . Wait! I won't let it in.

ELLA:

Well, read it . . .   230

GANUS:

            And let it in? Read it? So that
the old pain can unfurl itself once more?
Once you asked me, should you go . . . Now
I ask you, shall I read it? Shall I?

ELLA:

                  I answer: no.

GANUS:

You're right! There! To shreds . . . And put this heap
of dried falling stars here . . . under the table . . .   235
in the basket woven with a coat-of-arms . . .
My hands smell of perfume . . . There . . . It's over.

ELLA:

Oh, how bright it is today! . . . The spring
shines through . . . Chirruping. The snow is melting.
There are droplets on the black branches . . .   240
Let's go, let's go, for a walk, Ganus? Do you
want to?

GANUS:

        Yes, Ella, yes! I am free,
free! Let's go.

ELLA:

            You wait here . . . I'll go
get dressed . . . I won't be long . . .
    [*Leaves.*]

GANUS [*alone, looking out of the window*]:

                Yes, truly,
it is wonderful; a beautiful day! A pigeon   245
flew by there . . . Brightness, dampness . . . wonderful!

A workman forgot his spade . . . Somehow she lives
out there, at her sister's, in that distant place . . .
Does she know of his death? . . . Begone, you
250   cunning devil! Because of you, I destroyed
my homeland . . . Enough! I hate this woman . . .
Come back to me, O music of repentance!
Prayers, prayers . . . I am free, I am free . . .
> [*Slowly* TREMENS *and the four* REBELS *return, with* KLIAN
> *behind them.*]

FIRST REBEL:
Be more careful, Tremens, don't be angry,
255   understand, you must be more careful!
It's a dangerous path . . . You yourself have
heard: under torture they sang of the King . . .
ever more finely, ever more blissfully . . .
The King is a dream . . . The King has not died
260   in their souls, merely grown quiet . . . the dream
folded its wings—a moment—and now extends them . . .

KLIAN:
My leader, it's gone eight; the city is awake,
it stirs . . . The people call you to the square . . .

TREMENS:
Coming, coming . . .
> [*to the* FIRST REBEL]
                So what are you saying?

FIRST REBEL:
265   I'm saying that a winged legend flies,
turning in the sun! Mothers whisper
the fairy tale to their children . . . Beggars
speak of the King over home-brewed beer . . .
How can you outlaw the wind itself?
270   You are too angry, too merciless.
It's a dangerous path! Be more careful,

we ask, there's nothing stronger than a dream! . . .

TREMENS:

I'll break its neck! You dare to teach me? I'll break it!
Or, perhaps, the dream is dear to you?

SECOND REBEL:

You have misunderstood us, Tremens,   275
we wanted to warn you . . .

KLIAN:

The King is nothing but
a straw scarecrow . . .

TREMENS:

Enough! Leave me, you
woeful cowards! Ganus, well then, have you . . .
decided?

GANUS:

Tremens, truly, do not torment me . . .
You know yourself. I want only prayer,   280
only prayer . . .

TREMENS:

Leave, and quickly!
I have suffered you too long . . . Everything
has its limit . . . Help him, Klian—he can't
open the door, he's pulling at it . . .

KLIAN:

Here,
let me—towards yourself . . .   285

GANUS:

. . . But perhaps
she's calling for me! Oh!
[*Throws himself at a table.*]

KLIAN:

Wait . . . Calm down . . .
Save yourself, Tremens, he's . . .

GANUS:

Let go! Just don't
touch me, do you understand? There's no need
to touch me . . . Where's the basket? Move away!
290   The basket! . . .

TREMENS:

He's mad . . .

GANUS:

Here . . . in pieces . . .
in my palms . . . silver . . . Oh, that impetuous
handwriting!

[*reads*]

Here . . . here . . . "my fan . . . send me . . .
He's worn me out" . . . Who's he? Who's he? The pieces
are all jumbled up . . . "Forgive me" . . . That's not it.
295   That's not it either . . . Some address . . . strange . . .
in the south . . .

KLIAN:

Shall I call the guard?

GANUS:

Tremens! . . .
Listen . . . Tremens! It must be I see things
differently from everyone else . . . Take a look . . .
After the words "and I'm unhappy" . . . That name . . .
300   See it? That name there . . . Can you make it out?

TREMENS:

"Mark is with me"—no, not Mark . . . "Morn,"
is it? Morn . . . That sounds familiar . . . Ah,
I've remembered! How glorious! That's fate
for you! So that buffoon tricked you?
305   Where are you going? Wait . . .

GANUS:

Morn lives,
God is dead. That's all . . . I go to kill Morn.

TREMENS:

Wait . . . No, no, don't pull away . . .
I've had enough . . . You hear? I talked to you
of chasms, of giants—and you . . . how dare you
bring in here the spirit of masquerade,   310
the babble of life, the squeak of mousy passion?
Wait . . . I am tired of you putting your . . . anguish—
your heart, that ace of hearts pierced by an arrow,—
above my, my thunderous worlds!
Enough of your living in this anguish!   315
I am jealous! No, lift up your face!
Look, look into my eyes, as into a grave.
So, you wish to assuage your fate? Stop
pulling away! Listen, do you remember
a certain happy evening? The eight of clubs?   320
Know, then, that it was I—cursed Tremens—
that your fate . . .

ELLA [*in the doorway*]:

Father, leave him be!

TREMENS:

. . . your fate . . . I pity . . . Leave. Hey, somebody!
He's grown faint—take him under the elbows!

GANUS:

Be off, you ravens! The corpse of Morn—is mine!   325
[*Leaves.*]

TREMENS:

Close the door behind him, Klian. Tightly.
There's a draught.

SECOND REBEL [*quietly*]:

                I said there was a lover . . .

FIRST REBEL:

Quiet, I'm feeling frightened . . .

THIRD REBEL:

                      How Tremens frowns.

SECOND REBEL:

Unhappy Ganus . . .

FOURTH REBEL:

                He's happier than us . . .

KLIAN [*loudly*]:

330   My leader! I shall dare to repeat myself.
The people are gathered in the square. They wait
for you.

TREMENS:

          I know . . . Hey, follow me, you sheep!
Why have you gone so quiet? Look lively!
I will give such a speech, that tomorrow

335   nothing but ashes will remain of the city.
No, Klian, you aren't to come with us:
your neck hints too much of the gallows.

    [TREMENS *and the* REBELS *leave.* ELLA *and* KLIAN *remain*
    onstage.]

KLIAN:

Did you hear that? Your father is a splendid
joker. I like it. It's funny.

    [*Pause.*]

                Ella, you have

340   a white hat on—are you going somewhere?

ELLA:

Nowhere. I've changed my mind . . .

KLIAN:

My wife
is beautiful. I don't find time to tell you that
you are beautiful. Only from time to time,
in my poems . . .

ELLA:

I don't understand them.
[*Screams are heard offstage.*]

KLIAN:

Hark! The howl of the crowd . . . That welcoming peal!   345

CURTAIN

A drawing room in a southern villa. A glass door onto a terrace, lead-
ing out to a fantastical garden. In the middle of the stage is a table set
with three places. A foul spring morning. MIDIA *stands with her back*
to the audience, looking out of the window. Somewhere a servant
strikes a gong. The noise dies down. MIDIA *doesn't move.* EDMIN
enters from the left with the newspapers.

EDMIN:

    Again there is no sun . . . How did you sleep?

MIDIA:

    On my back, and on my side, and even
    in the foetal position . . .

EDMIN:

                       Are we taking
    coffee in the drawing room?

MIDIA:

                   Yes,
    as you can see. The dining room is gloomy.

EDMIN:

    The news is even more terrible than before . . .
    These are not newspapers, but shrouds
    drenched with death, with the dankness of the grave . . .

MIDIA:

    They must have got wet in the postman's bag.

10   It has rained since morning, the gravel is dark.

    And the palm trees have drooped.

EDMIN:

                      Here, listen:

    the suburbs are ablaze . . . the crowds have looted

    the museums . . . they light bonfires in the squares . . .

    And drink, and dance . . . Execution follows

15   execution . . . And into the drunken city

    has come the plague . . .

MIDIA:

                What do you think, will

    the rain stop soon? It's so dull . . .

EDMIN:

                 Meanwhile,

    their savage leader . . . You knew his daughter . . .

MIDIA:

                            Yes,

    I think so . . . I don't remember . . . What's death

20   to me, chaos, blood, when I'm so bored

    that I don't know what to do with myself!

    Oh, Edmin, he has given up shaving,

    he walks around in his dressing gown,

    he's gloomy, and abrupt, and stubborn . . .

25   It's as though we've crossed from a fairy tale

    to the most banal reality . . . He is becoming

    duller, has started hunching his shoulders,

    ever since we came to live here, in this swamp . . .

    The palm trees, you know, always remind me

30   of the hallways of rich merchants . . . Edmin,

    leave the newspapers . . . It's nonsense . . . You are

always so reserved with me, as though
I were a whore or a queen . . .

EDMIN:

                              Not at all . . .
I only . . . You do not know, Midia, what
you are doing! . . . O, God, what is there   35
for us to talk about?

MIDIA:

                        I loved his laughter:
he laughs no longer . . . While once it seemed
to me that this tall, happy, quick-witted man
must be some kind of artist, a wondrous
genius, concealing his visions for the sake   40
of my jealous love,—and in not knowing
there lay for me a blissful thrill . . . Now I
have understood that he is dull and empty,
that my dream does not live in him,
that his light has gone out, he has fallen   45
out of love with me . . .

EDMIN:

                        You mustn't bewail
things so . . . Who could fall out of love with you?
You are so . . . well, enough—come on, smile!
Your smile is the movement of an angel . . .
I beg you! . . . Today, even your fingers are   50
motionless . . . They too do not smile . . . Ah, there! . . .

MIDIA:

Has it been long?

EDMIN:

                    Has what been long, Midia?

MIDIA:

Well. That's interesting . . . I've never seen you

like this. No, in fact, I did once ask you
55   what the point was of your standing guard
in the street . . .

EDMIN:

                I remember, remember
only the curtain in your tormenting window!
You swam past in the embraces of another . . .
In the snowstorm I cried . . .

MIDIA:

                     How funny you are . . .
60   All dishevelled . . . Let me smooth your hair!
There. Now do my fingers laugh? Leave me . . .
oh, leave me . . . don't . . .

EDMIN:

                My happiness . . . allow me to . . .
just your lips . . . just touch . . . like touching fluff,
the wingbeat of a butterfly . . . allow me . . . happiness . . .

MIDIA:

65   But no . . . wait . . . we're by the window . . . the gardener . . .

. . . .

MIDIA:

My little one . . . don't breathe like that . . . Wait,
show me your eyes. Like that, closer . . . closer . . .
My soul would do nothing but bask and swim
70   in their soft darkness . . . Wait . . . more quietly . . .
later . . . There now! My hair comb's slipped . . .

EDMIN:

                          My life,
my love . . .

MIDIA:

           You are so little . . . So, so
little . . . You are a silly little boy . . .

What, did you not think I could kiss that way?
Wait, you will have time yet, for you and I   75
will leave for some enormous, noisy city
and will dine on the rooftop . . . You know,
below us, in the dark, will be the whole city,
all in lights; coolness, night . . . The rosy
reflection of a glass on the tablecloth . . . And   80
a frenzied fiddler, now all hunched up, now
raising his fiddle to the heavens! Will you
take me away? Will you? Ah . . . shuffling . . .
let me go . . . it's him . . . move away . . .

    [MISTER MORN *enters, in a dark robe, dishevelled.*]

MORN:

Night? Day? I do not notice the shift.   85
Morning is a continuation of sleeplessness.
My temples ache. As though someone has pressed,
screwed into my head a cast-iron cube.
Today I shall take coffee without milk . . .

    [*Pause.*]

Again, the newspapers are scattered all over   90
the place! Why . . . you are cheerless, Edmin! . . .
How astonishing: I need only enter
and immediately there are long faces—
like shadows in the evening sun . . . Strange . . .

MIDIA:

It is a foul spring . . .   95

MORN:

                I am to blame.

MIDIA:

. . . And the news is dreadful . . .

MORN:

                    And I am to blame
for that too, is that not so?

MIDIA:

> The city burns.
> Everything has gone mad. I don't know
> how it will end . . . Yet they say the King's
> 100   not dead, but is walled up underground
> by the rebels . . .

MORN:

> Eh, Midia, that will do!
> You know, I will forbid the newspapers
> to be brought. I have no peace from these
> conjectures; rumours, news of bloodshed
> 105   and idle gossip. I've had enough! Trust me,
> Midia, you need not try to be clever
> in front of me . . . Be bored, anguished, change
> your hairstyle, your dresses, lengthen your eyes
> with a blue line, look in the mirror—but don't
> 110   try to be clever . . . What's wrong with you, Edmin?

EDMIN [*rises from the table*]:

> I can't . . .

MORN:

> What's wrong with him? What's wrong with him?
> Where are you going? It's damp on the terrace . . .

MIDIA:

> Leave him. I shall tell you everything. Listen,
> I too can take no more. I am in love
> 115   with him. I am leaving with him. You will
> get used to it. Really, you don't need me.
> We would torment each other. Life calls . . .
> I need happiness . . .

MORN:

> I understand—where
> is the sugar bowl? . . . Ah, here it is.
> 120   Under the napkin.

MIDIA:

So then, you do not wish
to listen? . . .

MORN:

No, on the contrary—
I am listening . . . grasping, comprehending,
what more can I do? Do you wish to leave
today?

MIDIA:

Yes.

MORN:

I think it's about time
you started packing.

MIDIA:

Yes. Don't hurry me.

MORN:

According to the rules of separation,
you must still throw over your shoulder the phrase:
"I curse the day . . ."

MIDIA:

You never loved . . . You never
loved! . . . Yes, I have the right to curse
that faithless day, when your laugh entered
my quiet house . . . Why did you . . .

MORN:

By the way,
tell me, Midia, did you write to your husband
from here?

MIDIA:

I . . . I thought—it was not worth
reporting . . . Yes, I wrote to my husband.

MORN:

What exactly? Look me in the eyes.

125

130

135

MIDIA:

Nothing,
really . . . That I ask forgiveness, that you are
here with me, that I won't go back to him . . .
that it rains here . . .

MORN:

And you sent your address?

MIDIA:

Yes, I think . . . Asked him to send my fan . . .
140   I forgot it there, at home . . .

MORN:

And when
did you send it?

MIDIA:

About two weeks ago.

MORN:

Wonderful . . .

MIDIA:

I'll go . . . I need to . . . my things . . .
[*Leaves to the right.* MORN *is alone. Through the glass door, on
the terrace, the motionless back of* EDMIN *can be seen.*]

MORN:

Wonderful . . . Ganus, having received the letter,
will remind me of my debt. He'll force his way
145   out of the haze of the maddened city, out
of the mangled fairy tale, here, to the grey
south, into my hollow, humdrum existence.
Not long to wait. He must be on his way.
We shall meet once more, and, handing me
150   the pistol, he, clenched and pale, will demand
that I should kill myself, and I shall, perhaps,
be ready: death ripens in solitude . . .

I am

amazed . . . Life has forsaken me so abruptly.
But I mustn't think of my homeland,—
or I'll end up rushing around a dungeon   155
with padded mattresses instead of walls and
with the number of madness above the door . . .
I don't believe it . . . How else to live? Edmin!
Come here! . . . Edmin, do you hear? Your hand,
give me your hand . . . My faithful friend, thank you.   160

EDMIN:

What can I say? Not blood but a cold shame
flows through my veins. I feel that you must now
look into my eyes as one looks at those
dirty pictures, that for a tuppence you can
gawp at through a peep-hole . . . My heart is full   165
of shame . . .

MORN:

No, it's nothing . . . I am only astonished . . .
Death is an astonishment. In life, too,
we are sometimes astonished: the ocean, the colour
of a cloud, the twist of fate . . . It is
as though I am standing on my head. I see   170
everything the way, they say, that babies see it:
the candle flame, tip pointing downwards . . .

EDMIN:

My sovereign, what can I say to you? You
betrayed a kingdom for a woman, I
betrayed a friendship for a woman—the very   175
same one . . . Forgive me. I am only human,
my sovereign . . .

MORN:

And I, I am Mister Morn—
that is all; an empty space, an unstressed

syllable in a poem without rhyme.
180   Oh, no one would have been unfaithful
to the King . . . But—to Mister Morn . . .
You should go. I have understood—this
is retribution. I'm not angry. But leave.
It is hard for me to talk with you. Only
185   a moment, and it is as though one has
shaken the coloured glass inside a tube,
glanced through it—and life has changed . . .
Farewell. Be happy.

EDMIN:

I will come back to you,
if you but call . . .

MORN:

I will meet you only
190   in heaven. No earlier. There, in the shade
of an olive tree, I'll introduce you to Brutus.
Go . . .

[EDMIN *leaves.*]

MORN [*alone*]:

Well. It's over.

[*Pause. A* SERVANT *enters.*]

MORN:

The table needs
to be cleared. Hurry up . . . Is the carriage
ordered?

SERVANT:

Yes, sir.

MORN:

Tomorrow morning,
195   have the barber come from the town—
the moustached, silent one. That is all.

[*The* SERVANT *leaves. Pause.* MORN *looks out of the window.*]

MORN:

> > > The sky
> is murky. The flowers tremble in the garden . . .
> The artificial grotto blackens: the rain
> stretches out in strings against the black . . .
> Only one thing is left now: to await   200
> Ganus. My soul is almost ready. How
> the wet greenery shines . . . The rain quivers
> as though in senile drowsiness . . . The house
> meanwhile has awoken . . . The servants bustle . . .
> The trunks clatter . . . And here she is . . .   205
> > [*Enter* MIDIA *with an open suitcase.*]

MORN:

> > > > Midia,
> are you happy?

MIDIA:

> > > Yes. Move. I need
> to pack these . . .

MORN:

> > > A familiar suitcase:
> I carried it once at dawn. The snow crunched.
> And the three of us were hurrying.

MIDIA:

> These things go in it—books, portraits . . .   210

MORN:

> That's fine . . . Midia, are you happy?

MIDIA:

> There's a train at midday exactly: I shall
> fly away to a marvellous foreign city . . .
> I wish I had some paper—this might break . . .
> And whose is this? Yours? Mine? I don't   215
> recall, I don't recall . . .

MORN:

Only don't cry,
I beg you . . .

MIDIA:

Yes, yes . . . you are right.
It has passed . . . I won't . . . I didn't know
that you would let me go so easily,
220 so willingly . . . I jerked the door open . . .
I thought you held the handle tightly on
the other side . . . I jerked it open with all
my might,—you were not holding it, the door
opened easily, and I fell back . . . You
225 understand, I am falling . . . In my eyes
there is rippled darkness, and I think
I will perish—I cannot find a foothold! . . .

MORN:

Edmin is with you. He is happiness . . .

MIDIA:

I don't
know anything! . . . Only it's strange: we loved—
230 and it has all gone somewhere. We loved . . .

MORN:

These two engravings here are yours, aren't they?
And this porcelain dog?

MIDIA:

. . . It's strange . . .

MORN:

No, Midia.
In harmony there is nothing strange. And life
is a vast harmony. I've understood this.
235 But, you see—the moulded whimsy of a frieze
on a portico keeps us from recognizing,
sometimes, the symmetry of the whole . . .

You will leave; we'll forget one another;
but now and then the name of a street,
or a street organ weeping in the twilight,   240
will remind us in a more vivid and more
truthful way than thought could resurrect
or words convey, of that main thing
which was between us, the main thing which
we do not know . . . And in that hour, the soul   245
will miraculously sense the charm
of past trifles, and we will understand
that in eternity all is eternal—
the genius's thought and the neighbour's
joke, the bewitched suffering of Tristan   250
and the most fleeting love . . . Let us part
without bitterness, Midia: some day, perhaps,
you will discover the unspoken reason
for my deep sorrow, my cold anguish . . .

MIDIA:

I dreamt, at the beginning, that beneath   255
the laughter you were hiding a secret . . . So,
there is a secret?

MORN:

        Shall I reveal it to you?
Will you believe it?

MIDIA:

        I shall.

MORN:

        So listen then:
when we saw one another in the city,
I was—how shall I say?—an enchanter,   260
a hypnotist . . . I read thoughts . . . I
predicted fate, twirling my crystal;
beneath my fingers the oak table rocked

like the deck of a ship, and the dead sighed,
265   spoke through my larynx, and the kings
of bygone ages inhabited me . . .
Now I have lost my gift . . .

MIDIA:

                    And that is all?

MORN:

That is all. Are you taking these music scores
with you? Let me squeeze them in—no,
270   they don't fit. And this book? Hurry, Midia,
there is less than an hour till the train . . .

MIDIA:

                            Well . . .

I am ready . . .

MORN:

            Here they come with your trunk.
One more. Coffins . . .

    [*Pause.*]

               Well then, farewell, Midia,
be happy . . .

MIDIA:

           I keep thinking I have forgotten
275   something . . . Tell me—were you joking about
the spinning tables?

MORN:

              I don't remember . . . I don't
remember . . . it doesn't matter . . . Farewell. Go.
He is waiting for you. Don't cry.

    [*They both go out onto the terrace.*]

MIDIA:

                   Forgive me . . .
We loved—and it has all gone, somewhere . . .
280   We loved—and now our love is frozen,

and now it lies, one wing spread out, raising
its little feet—a dead sparrow on the damp
gravel . . . But we loved . . . we flew . . .

MORN:

                        Look,
the sun is coming out . . . Watch your step—
it's slippery here, be careful . . . Farewell . . .   285
farewell . . . Remember . . . Remember only
the shimmer on the tree trunk, the rain, the sun . . .
only that . . .

    [*Pause.* MORN *is on the terrace alone. We see him slowly turn
    his face from left to right, as he follows with his gaze those
    departing. Then he returns to the drawing room.*]

MORN:

            Well. It is over . . .
    [*He wipes his head with a handkerchief.*]
The flying rain has settled in my hair.
    [*Pause.*]
I fell in love with her at the very moment,   290
when, at a street corner, her hat flashed past,
the wet wing of a carriage—and disappeared
into an avenue of cypresses . . . Now I'm
alone. The end. And so, having deceived
destiny, thrown my crown to the Devil
for his sport, and yielded my belovèd   295
to a friend . . .
    [*Pause.*]
              How quietly she went down
those steps, putting the same foot forward
every time—like a child . . . Be still,
my heart! A hot, hot shriek, a howl,   300
rises, grows in my chest . . . No! No!
There is a way: to stare at the mirror,

to hold back the sobs that turn my face
into a toad's . . . Oh! I cannot . . .
305   In an empty house and eye to eye
with the cold angel of my sleepless conscience . . .
How do I live? What do I do? My God . . .
    [*Cries.*]
Well . . . well . . . I feel better. That was Morn
crying; the King is absolutely calm.
310   I feel better . . . Those tears removed the speck
caught in my eye—the point of pain. I will
not wait for Ganus, after all . . . My soul
is growing, my soul gains in strength—preparing
for death is like preparing for a holiday . . .
315   But let the preparations go on in secret.
Soon it will be day—I will not wait
for Ganus after all—day will break,
and lightly I will kill myself. One cannot
summon death with a strained thought; death
320   shall come itself, and I will pull the trigger
as if by accident . . . Yes, I feel better—
perhaps it is the sun, shining through
the slanted rain . . . or tenderness—younger
sister of death—that mute, radiant tenderness
325   that rises up when a woman leaves forever . . .
She's forgotten to push in these drawers . . .
    [*walks around, tidying things*]
. . . The books have fallen over on their sides,
as thoughts do, when sadness pulls one out
and carries it off: the one about God . . .
330   The piano is open on a barcarole:
she loved elegant sounds . . . The little table,
like a meadow mowed: here there was
a portrait of her family, of someone else,

cards, some kind of jewellery box . . .
She took everything . . . And, as in the song—   335
I have been left with only these roses here:
their crumpled edges slightly touched with
tender mildew, and in the tall vase the water
smells of rot, of death, as it does
under ancient bridges. I am stirred, roses,   340
by your honeyed decay . . . You need fresh water.
[*Goes out by the door on the right. The stage is empty for some
time. Then—quick, pale, in tattered clothes—*GANUS *enters
from the terrace.*]

GANUS:

Morn . . . Morn . . . where's Morn? By a stony path,
through bushes . . . some kind of garden . . . and now—
I'm in his drawing room . . . This is a dream,
but before I wake up . . . It's quiet here . . .   345
Can he have left? What should I do? Wait?
Lord, Lord, Lord, allow me to meet
with him alone! . . . I will take aim and fire . . .
And it will be over! . . . Who is that? . . . Oh,
only the reflection of a ragged fellow . . .   350
I am afraid of mirrors . . . What shall I do
next? My hand trembles,—it was unwise
to drink wine there, in that tavern,
beneath the hill . . . And there's a din in my ears.
But, perhaps? Yes, definitely! The rustle   355
of footsteps . . . Now quick . . . Where should I . . .
[*And he hides to the left, behind the corner of a cupboard,
having pulled out his pistol.* MORN *returns. He fusses over the
flowers on the table, with his back to* GANUS. GANUS, *stepping
forward, aims with a trembling hand.*]

MORN:

Oh, you poor things . . . breathe, flame up . . .

You resemble love. You were made
for similes; it is not for nothing that from
360   the first days of the universe there has flowed
through your petals the blood of Apollo . . . An ant . . .
Funny: he runs, like a man amidst a fire . . .

    [GANUS *takes aim.*]

CURTAIN

Scene I

Old DANDILIO'*s room. A cage with a parrot, books, porcelain. Through the windows—a sunny summer's day.* KLIAN *charges around the room. In the distance gunshots can be heard.*

KLIAN:
It seems to be getting quieter . . . All the same,
I'm doomed! The lead will strike into my brain
like a stone into glistening mud—an instant—
and my thoughts will splatter out! If only
5   it were possible to juicily belch up the life
one's lived, chew it anew and gulp it down,
and then once more to roll it with a fat,
ox-like tongue, to squeeze from its eternal
dregs the former sweetness of crisp grass,
10   drunk with the morning dew and the bitterness
of lilac leaves! O, God, if only one could
always feel deathly terror! That, God,
would be bliss! Every terror signifies
"I am," and there's no higher bliss! Terror—
15   but not the stillness of the grave! The groans
of suffering—but not the silence of the corpse!
This is wisdom, there can be no other!
I am prepared, having strummed my lyre,

to break it, to give up my melodious gift,
to become a leper, to weaken, to grow deaf,—   20
if only to remember some little thing, be it
the rustle of nails scratching a sore,—to me
that is sweeter than the songs of the otherworld!
I'm frightened, death nears . . . My taut heart
lurches heavily, like a sack in a cart, clattering   25
downhill, towards a cliff, towards an abyss!
It can't be stopped! Death!

    [DANDILIO *enters from a door on the right.*]

DANDILIO:

                    Hush, hush, hush . . .
Ella has only just fallen asleep in there;
the poor thing lost a lot of blood; the child
is dead and the mother has lost her second   30
soul—the dearer one. But she seems better . . .
Only, you know, I am no doctor—I used
what books I had, but still . . .

KLIAN:

                    Dandilio!
My dear Dandilio! My wonderful, my radiant
Dandilio! . . . I cannot, I cannot . . .   35
for they will catch me here! I am doomed!

DANDILIO:

I must confess, I was not expecting such
guests; you could have warned me yesterday:
I would have decorated the parrot's cage—
he's very gloomy for some reason. Tell me,   40
Klian—I was busy with Ella, I didn't fully
understand—how was it that you escaped
with her?

KLIAN:

        I am doomed! How awful . . .
What a night! They forced their way . . . Ella
45   kept asking where the child was . . . The crowds
broke into the palace . . . We were overcome:
for five terrifying days we fought against
the hurricane that was the people's dream;
last night all fell to ruins: they hunted us
50   through the palace—myself and Tremens,
others too . . . I ran, with Ella in my arms,
from hall to hall, through inner galleries,
and back again, and up and down, and heard
the howls, the shots, and once or twice Tremens's
55   cold laugh . . . How Ella moaned, how she moaned!
Suddenly—a scrap of curtain, a chink behind it,—
I tugged: a passage! You understand—a secret
passage . . .

DANDILIO:

        Of course I understand . . . It was,
I should think, needed by the King,
60   so he could fly away unnoticed—and,
then, after his winged adventures, return
to his labours . . .

KLIAN:

          . . . and so I stumbled
in the sepulchral darkness, and walked and walked . . .
Suddenly—a wall: I pushed—and found myself
65   miraculously in an empty alley!
Only a gunshot sounded from time to time
and tore the air at its seam . . . I remembered
you live nearby—and so . . . we came to you . . .
But what shall we do next? To stay with you

would be madness! They will find me! Indeed, 70
the whole city knows you were once friendly
with mad Tremens, and christened his daughter! . . .
DANDILIO:
She is weak: she won't survive another
such excursion. But where is Tremens?
KLIAN:

He fights . . .
I don't know where . . . He himself advised me, 75
the day before, that I bring my sick Ella
to you . . . but it is dangerous here, I
am doomed! Understand,—I don't know how,
I don't know how to die, and it's too late—
I won't learn now, there is no time! They're 80
coming for me now! . . .
DANDILIO:

Flee alone.
You still have time. I'll give you a false
beard and glasses and you'll be on your way.
KLIAN:
You think so?
DANDILIO:

Or if you want, I have the masks
that people used to wear on Shrovetide 85
in bygone days . . .
KLIAN:

. . . Yes, you may mock!
You know yourself that I will never abandon
my weak Ella . . . That's where the horror lies—
not in death, no,—but in the fact that some
sort of whimpering feeling has inhabited 90
my blood, a mixture of untold jealousy

and shunned desire, and such tenderness
that all sunsets are but puddles of paint
beside it—such is my tenderness!
95   No one knew! I am a coward, a viper,
a flatterer, but here, in this . . .

DANDILIO:

                         Enough, friend . . .
Calm down . . .

KLIAN:

                Love has squeezed my heart
in its palms . . . holds it . . . won't let it go . . .
If I pull it—it contracts . . . But death
100   is near . . . yet how can I tear myself
from my own heart? I'm not a lizard, I can't
grow it back . . .

DANDILIO:

               You're rambling, calm down:
it's safe here . . . The street is sunny and deserted . . .
Where is death to be seen? On the spines
105   of my sleepy books there is a smile.
And my blessèd parrot is calm as a vision.

KLIAN:

    That bird dazzles my eyes . . . Please understand,
they will descend upon us now—there is
no way out! . . .

DANDILIO:

               I sense no danger:
110   a blind rumour blown in from the south,
that the King is alive, has intoxicated
souls with an unheard-of joy; the city is so
tired of executions that, having finished
with Tremens, the chief madman, they will
115   hardly start searching for his accomplices.

KLIAN:

You think so? Yes, it's true, the sun is shining . . .
And the gunshots have died down . . . Shall I open
the window, shall I look out? Eh?

DANDILIO:

                         Moreover,
I have this little thing . . . shall I show you?
Here, in this soft case . . . My talisman . . .   120
Here, look . . .

KLIAN:

           The crown!

DANDILIO:

                Wait, you'll drop it . . .

KLIAN:

Do you hear? . . . O, God . . . Someone . . . On the stairs . . .
Ah!

DANDILIO:

    I said you'd drop it!
    [*Enter* TREMENS.]

TREMENS:

              Golden thunder!
I'm touched! But in vain were you preparing
to crown me. Congratulate me, Klian: half   125
a kingdom is promised for my bald pate! . . .
    [*to* DANDILIO]
Tell me, blithe old man, when and how
did you come by that piece of lustre?

DANDILIO:

                   One
of those who searched the palace sold it to me
for a gold coin.   130

TREMENS:

Well, well . . . Give it here. It fits.
But I confess, right now, I would prefer
a nightcap. Where is Ella?

DANDILIO:

Nearby. She's sleeping.

TREMENS:

Ah . . . good. Klian, why are you whining?

KLIAN:

I can't . . . Tremens, Tremens, why did I follow
135   you? You are death, you are the abyss!
We will both perish.

TREMENS:

You're absolutely right.

KLIAN:

My friend, my leader . . . You are the wisest of all.
Save me—and Ella . . . Teach me—what should
I do? . . . My Tremens, what should I do?

TREMENS:

140   What should you do? Sleep. I shiver once more;
once more that naked concubine—fever—
clings to my stomach with her cold thighs,
strokes, strokes my back with her icy palms . . .
Give me something to throw over my shoulders,
145   old man. That's it. Yes, my dear Klian,
I am convinced that our friends were right
when they warned us that . . . By the way,
I executed all four of them—
they tried to betray me . . . All I needed!
150   I am going to sleep. Let the soldiers
find me themselves.

KLIAN: [*cries out*]:

Ah! . . .

DANDILIO:

                                Don't shout . . .
don't. There. I knew that would happen.
   [ELLA *enters from the right.*]

TREMENS:

My daughter, Ella, do not fear: all is well!
Klian here is singing his latest poems . . .

ELLA:

Father, are you wounded? There's blood.   155

TREMENS:

                             No.

ELLA:

Your hand is once more, once more cold . . .
and your nails, they look as though you've eaten
wild strawberries . . . I will stay here, Dandilio . . .
I will lie down, give me a pillow . . . Really,
I feel better . . . All night they fired . . . My child   160
cried . . . But where is your cat, Dandilio? . . .

DANDILIO:

Some prankster struck it with a stone bottle . . .
Otherwise I would not have bought the parrot . . .

ELLA:

Yes, the fiery one . . . Yes, I do
recall . . . We drank to its health . . . Ah!   165
   [*laughs*]
"And yet I fear you . . . For you are fatal then . . ."
—where is that from? Where's it from? No,
I have forgotten.

KLIAN:

               Enough . . . Ella . . . my love . . .
close your eyes . . .

ELLA:

              . . . You are as pale as a fresh

170   pine-board . . . and droplets of resin . . . I don't
    like it . . . Go away . . .

KLIAN:

                          Forgive me . . . I won't, I just . . .
    I wanted to fix your pillow . . . There . . .
    [*He sinks down at her bedside.*]

TREMENS:

    What was I saying? Yes, they search badly;
    there, around the senate, around the palace,
175   the people crowd about, cleaning the royal
    chambers, airing the carpets, and sweeping up
    my cigarette butts and Ella's hairpins . . .
    Very amusing! And what an amusing rumour,
    that apparently a burglar—somewhere in the south,
180   you see—climbed into the house and whacked
    the owner on the head—who, in turn,
    if you please, turned out to be that very ruler
    who abandoned his city half a year ago . . .
    I know, I know, these are all fantasies. But
185   with just such a fantasy they swept me aside.
    There, Ella sleeps. It's also time for me . . .
    The chill strokes, creeps up my back . . . But
    it's a shame, Dandilio, that the imaginary
    thief did not destroy the made-up king! . . .
190   You laugh? Do I joke well?

DANDILIO:

                        Yes, poor Ganus!
    He was unlucky . . .

TREMENS:

                  What do you mean—Ganus?

DANDILIO:

    Well, he received the letter . . . Ella told me . . .

How well the poor girl sleeps . . . Klian,
cover her feet with something . . .

TREMENS:

                Listen, listen,
Dandilio, perhaps amongst your antique toys,   195
your dusty knick-knacks, your magic books,
you have half a dozen good warm shirts?
Lend them to me . . .

DANDILIO:

             I would have given them
to you sooner, but they would have been
too small for you . . . What is it you want to say?   200

TREMENS:

Once, Dandilio, we were friends, we argued
about art . . . Then I became a widower . . .
Then the revolt—the first one—enthralled me,
and we met less frequently . . . I am not inclined
to idle sentimentality, but in the name   205
of that distant friendship, I ask you,
tell me clearly, what do you know of the King! . . .

DANDILIO:

What, have you not understood? It was all
so simple. Once, four years ago, having
come to your house, I lingered in the hall   210
amongst the coat-hangers, in the rough darkness,
and two people entered; I heard their quick
whispers: "My sovereign, it is dangerous, he is
an unrestrained rebel . . ." The other laughed
in response and whispered: "You wait downstairs,   215
I won't be long." And again quiet laughter . . .
I hid. After a minute, he left and, slapping
his glove, ran down the stairs—your carefree guest . . .

TREMENS:

I recall . . . of course . . . How did I not connect . . .

DANDILIO:

220   You were immersed in dusky thoughts. I kept
silent. We saw each other rarely: I don't like
cold and gloomy people. But I remembered . . .
Four years passed—I still remembered; and then,
when I met Morn at those recent parties,
225   I recognized the laughter of the King . . . Then,
when on the day of the duel you substituted . . .

TREMENS:

Wait, wait, you noticed that too?

DANDILIO:

                            Yes,
my eyes have grown used to chance details
in diligently tracing the trails of little beetles
230   and the scratches on the surface of antique
furniture, of peeling paint, the specks of dust
on nameless canvases.

TREMENS:

                   And you kept silent!

DANDILIO:

Of the two hearts, dearer to me was his
whose passion was keener. There is a third heart:
235   look—with what sorrow and tenderness,
not characteristic of him, does Klian
gaze on dreaming Ella, as though his fear
has gone to sleep with her . . .

TREMENS:

                  O, it amuses me
that, secretly from me, my very thought
240   and will had been at work, that after all,

I myself, with my own hand, sent death,
albeit an illusive one, to the King!
And secretly, I was not mistaken in Ganus:
he was the blind weapon of a blind man . . .
I don't complain! With a cold curiosity   245
I examine those cunning patterns—causes
and consequences—upon the bright blade
placed against my chest . . . I am happy
that, even for a moment, I taught people
the sweet anarchy of destruction . . . No,   250
my lesson will not pass without a trace!
That is to say, there is no thought, no
momentary weakness, which does not
reveal itself in a future action: the King
will clearly deceive again . . .   255

KLIAN:

                         You've woken up?
Sleep, Ella, sleep. It's frightening to think,
Ella . . .

TREMENS:

             O, it amuses me! If I had known
all this, I would have shouted to the people:
"Your king is a weak and shallow man. There is
no fairy tale, there's only Morn!"   260

DANDILIO:

                       Don't,
Tremens, be quiet . . .

ELLA:

                  Morn and . . . the King?
Is that what you said, father? The King in a blue
carriage,—no, not that . . . I danced with Morn—
no . . . wait . . . Morn . . .

DANDILIO:

Enough, he was joking . . .

TREMENS:

265   Klian, keep quiet, don't sob! . . . Listen, Ella . . .

DANDILIO:

Ella, can you hear us?

TREMENS:

Is her heart beating?

DANDILIO:

Yes. It will pass soon.

TREMENS:

Her eyes are open . . .
She can see. Ella! A pillar of salt . . . I didn't
know such fainting fits were possible . . .

KLIAN:

Voices!

270   In the street . . . It's them!

TREMENS:

Yes. We were expecting them . . .
Let's have a look . . .
    [*Opens the window.* VOICES *can be heard from the street
    below.*]

FIRST VOICE:

. . . the house.

SECOND VOICE:

Right! He can't get out.
Do we have all the exits?

FIRST VOICE:

All of them . . .

TREMENS:

May as well close it . . .
    [*Closes the window.*]

KLIAN [*rushing around*]:

Save me . . . quickly . . .
Dandilio . . . anywhere . . . I want to live . . . quick . . .
if only there was time . . . Ah!   275

[*Rushes out of the room through the door on the right.*]

TREMENS:

Could this be the end?

DANDILIO:

Yes, it seems so.

TREMENS:

I'll go out to them,
so Ella doesn't see. What do you feed
this orange bird?

DANDILIO:

He likes little ants' eggs,
raisins . . . Nice, isn't he? You know, try
the attic, and then the roof . . .   280

TREMENS:

No, I'll go.

I'm tired . . .

[*He goes towards the door, opens it, but the* CAPTAIN *and four
of his* SOLDIERS *push him back into the room.*]

CAPTAIN:

Stop! Get back!

TREMENS:

Yes, yes—
I am Tremens; but let's talk in the street . . .

CAPTAIN:

Get back. There.

[*to a* SOLDIER]

Search both of them.

[*to* DANDILIO]

Your name?

DANDILIO:

There, you've spilled my tobacco, oh dear!

285   Who looks for a man's name in his snuffbox?

May I offer you some?

CAPTAIN:

Are you the master here?

DANDILIO:

Indeed.

CAPTAIN:

And who is this?

DANDILIO:

A sick girl.

CAPTAIN:

You shouldn't have concealed a criminal here . . .

TREMENS [*with a yawn*]:

I ran in here by chance.

CAPTAIN:

Are you Tremens, the rebel?

TREMENS:

290   I want to sleep. Hurry . . .

CAPTAIN:

By the order issued

by the senate today, the nineteenth of June,

you are here and now to be . . . Hey! There is

someone else in there.

[*to the* SOLDIERS]

Hold them.

I'll take a look . . .

[*Leaves by the door on the right.* TREMENS *and* DANDILIO
talk amongst themselves, surrounded by mute, almost lifeless
SOLDIERS.]

TREMENS:
How he dawdles . . .

I want to sleep.   295

DANDILIO:
Yes, we shall soon sleep well . . .

TREMENS:
We? Please, they will not touch you.
Do you fear death?

DANDILIO:
I love all this: shadows,
light, the specks of dust in a ray of sunshine;
these pools of light on the floor; and large books
that smell of time. Death is curious, I don't   300
dispute . . .

TREMENS:
Ella's like a doll . . . What's wrong with her?

DANDILIO:
Yes, this won't do.

[*to a* SOLDIER]
Listen to me, my brother,
take this sick girl here to the bedroom, and after
we'll send for the doctor. What, are you deaf?

TREMENS:
Leave him. It's not necessary. They'll dispatch me,   305
somewhere to the side,—she won't even see.
Dandilio, you spoke of the sun . . . It's strange,
it seems to me we are alike, but in what way
I cannot comprehend . . . Let's settle it now.
Do you accept death?   310

DANDILIO:
Yes. Matter must decay
for matter to be resurrected—and from that,

the Trinity is clear to me. In what way?
Space is God, and matter is Jesus, and time
is the Holy Ghost. Hence my conclusion:
315   a world made up of these three,—our world—
is divine . . .

TREMENS:

             Yes, continue.

DANDILIO:

                     Do you hear
what trampling there is in my rooms? Those
are boots!

TREMENS:

           All the same, our world . . .

DANDILIO:

                             . . . is divine;
and therefore all is happiness; and so we must
320   all sing as we work: to live in this world
means to work for the master in three forms:
space, matter, and time. But the work ends
and we depart to the eternal feast, having
given our memory to time, our image
325   to space, and our love to matter.

TREMENS:

                        You see—
fundamentally I agree. But I don't need
the slavery of happiness. I rebel,
rebel against the master! Do you hear!
I call on all to drop their work! Head off
330   to the eternal feast: there in blissful
abysses we will rest.

DANDILIO:

                  They've caught him. A cry.

TREMENS:
> I had forgotten Klian . . .
> [KLIAN *bursts in from the right.*]

KLIAN:
> Ah! A trap!
>
> They're here too!
> [*Flings himself back into the room on the right.*]

ELLA [*raising herself up*]:
> Morn . . . Morn . . . Morn . . .
> It is as though I heard a voice in my sleep:
> Morn is the King . . . 335
> [*Becomes still again.*]

VOICE OF CAPTAIN [*in the room to the right, the door of which remains open*]:
> Enough of this rushing
> around the rooms!

VOICE OF KLIAN:
> I beg you . . .

VOICE OF CAPTAIN:
> Your name!

VOICE OF KLIAN:
> I beg you . . . I am young . . . I am so young!
> I am great, I am a genius! They don't
> kill geniuses! . . .

VOICE OF CAPTAIN
> Answer the question!

VOICE OF KLIAN:
> My name is Klian . . . But I will serve the King . . . 340
> I swear . . . I know where the crown is . . . I'll give it
> back . . . I swear . . .

VOICE OF CAPTAIN:
> Stop grabbing at my calves,
> I'll shoot a hole in my boot.

VOICE OF KLIAN:

Have merc— . . . !

[*A gunshot.* TREMENS *and* DANDILIO, *surrounded by motionless* SOLDIERS, *continue their conversation.*]

TREMENS:

Space is God, you say. Excellent. That is
345 the explanation for wings, those wings with which
we populate heaven . . .

VOICE OF KLIAN:

Ah! . . . There is no end,
no end . . .

VOICE OF CAPTAIN:

He's full of life, the wretch.

DANDILIO:

Yes.

We are stirred by swift flights, by wheels, sails,
and—in childhood—by games and, in our youth,
350 by dances.

[. . .]*

---

* Lines missing in the original Russian text, including "curtain" to mark the end of the scene.

Scene II

[MORN *and* EDMIN *with the* FOREIGNER *and other* GUESTS.]

[MORN]:
   [. . .]*
   Those killed by a bullet to the heart ought not
   to be beaten by gossip's petty pellets . . .
   This evening will be blue, like three hundred
   July days, condensed and thickened into darkness,
   creaking now with the urgent longing of toads   5
   on ponds, now with the convulsion of oily leaves . . .
   Had I not been King, I would have been a poet
   with a lyre hot in this night, saturated
   in blueness, in this vivid night, which quivers
   along its length under a swarm of stars,   10
   like the sensitive back of black Pegasus . . .
   But we shall not—shall we?—talk of death,
   —but with a bright conversation about
   the kingdom, about power, and about
   my happiness, you shall refresh my soul,   15
   chase from the light the long, soft butterflies—
   and gulp of wine will follow gulp, so that

---

* Lines missing in the original Russian text.

the words of the soul may sound more sweetly
and sincerely . . . I'm happy.

LADY:

Sovereign, will there

20   be dancing? . . .

MORN:

Dancing? There is no room to, Ella.

LADY:

My name is not Ella . . .

MORN:

I am mistaken . . .
so . . . I've remembered . . . I was saying there is
no room to dance here. But in the palace,
perhaps I will host a ball—an enormous one,

25   by candlelight, yes, by candlelight,
to the magnificent hum of an organ . . .

LADY:

The King . . . the King is laughing at me.

MORN:

I am happy! . . . And if I'm pale, it is from happiness! . . .
The bandage . . . it is too tight . . . Edmin, tell . . .

30   no, do it yourself . . . fix it . . . like that . . .
good . . .

GREY-HAIRED GUEST:

Perhaps the King is tired? Perhaps
the guests should . . .

MORN:

Oh, how alike he is! . . .
Look, Edmin—how alike! . . . No, I am not tired.
Have you been away from the city long?

GREY-HAIRED GUEST:

35   My sovereign, I was driven out by a storm:
the mob, having shied away from you,

accidentally pushed into me, almost crushing
my soul. I fled. Since then I have thought
and wandered. Now I will return, blessing
my sorrowful exile for the sweetness of return . . .   40
But in wine there are bees' wings; and in joy,
for me, there is a grief translucent: my old
house, where since childhood I have lived,
my house is burned . . .

EDMIN:

                     But the nation has been saved!

GREY-HAIRED GUEST:

How can I explain? A nation is a bodiless divinity,   45
whilst our favourite corner of our homeland—
that is the visible image of the bodiless.
We only know God by his parted beard;
we recognize our nation by the traits
of our dear home. No one can take God   50
or our homeland from us. But it's still sad
to lose the warm little image. My house
has perished. I weep.

MORN:

               I swear, I will build
that very same house in the very same spot
for you. And not an architect, but your love   55
will check the blueprints; your memories, not carpenters,
will aid me; not painters, but the alert eyes
of your childhood: in childhood we see the souls
of colours . . .

GREY-HAIRED GUEST:

             Sovereign, I thank you: I know
that you are a magician, I'm happy that   60
you've understood me, but I do not need
a home . . .

MORN:

        I made a vow . . . What's in a vow?
The babble of pride. And when you look, death
is always there. What's in a vow? Even
65   the star deceives the stargazer, by sometimes
not returning at the expected time.
Wait . . . Tell me . . . did you know that old man—
Dandilio?

GREY-HAIRED GUEST:

        Dandilio? No, sovereign, I don't recall . . .

SECOND VISITOR [*quietly*]:

Look at the King, he's displeased with something . . .

THIRD VISITOR [*quietly*]:

70   As though a shadow—the shadow of a bird—
flew across his bright, pale face . . . Who's that?
   [*There is movement to the left, by the door.*]

VOICE:

Excuse me . . . What is your name? You cannot
come in here!

FOREIGNER:

        I am a Foreigner . . .

VOICE:

                Wait!

FOREIGNER:

No . . . I shall come in . . . I'm just . . . I'm nothing.
75   I'm simply asleep . . .

VOICE:

        He's drunk, don't let him in! . . .

MORN:

Ah, a new guest! Come in, come in, quickly!
I am so happy that I'd welcome with a smile
even an angel mournfully dragging himself
beneath the funereal hump of his folded wings;

or a beggar with some brilliant trick;   80
or an executioner with his tidy frock-coat
tightly fastened . . . Well then, my dear guest,
approach!

FOREIGNER:

       They say you are the King?

EDMIN:

                        How dare you! . . .

MORN:

Leave him. He's foreign. Yes, I am the King . . .

FOREIGNER:

So, then . . . I'm pleased: I dreamt you up well . . .   85

MORN:

Keep silent, Edmin—it's amusing. Have you
come from afar, my nebulous guest?

FOREIGNER:

                              From
commonplace reality, from the dull real world . . .
I am asleep . . . All this is a dream . . . the dream
of a drunken poet . . . A recurring dream . . .   90
I dreamt of you once: some ball . . . some city . . .
frosty and merry . . . Only you had a different
name . . .

MORN:

    Morn?

FOREIGNER:

           Morn. That's it . . .
An elaborate dream . . . But you know,
I was glad to wake up . . . I remember something   95
wasn't right there. But what I don't recall . . .

MORN:

Does everyone in your country speak so . . .
dreamily?

FOREIGNER:

        Oh, no! In our country all is not well,
not well . . . When I wake up, I will tell them
100   what a magnificent king I dreamt of . . .

MORN:

Curious fellow!

FOREIGNER:

        But what makes me uneasy?
I don't know . . . Just like last time . . . I'm frightened . . .
My bedroom must be stuffy. Something fills me
with fear . . . an illusion . . . I'll try to wake up . . .

MORN:

105   Wait! . . . Where did my ghost slip off to? . . . Wait,
come back . . .

VOICE [*from the left*]:

        Hold him!

SECOND VOICE:

        I can't see him . . .

THIRD VOICE:

              Night . . .

EDMIN:

My sovereign, how can you bear to listen to that?

MORN:

Past kings had fools: they spoke the truth darkly,
cunningly—and the kings loved their fools . . .
110   While I have this spurious somnambulist . . .
Why have you grown quiet, dear guests?
Drink to my happiness! And you, Edmin.
Eh, brighten up! All drink! The heart of Bacchus
is like cut glass: in it is blood and sunshine . . .

GUESTS:

115   Long live the King!

MORN:

                    The King . . . the King . . .

Heavenly thunder rumbles in that earthly word.

So! We've drunk! Now I will hearten my subjects:

I intend to return tomorrow!

EDMIN:

                         Sovereign . . .

GUESTS:

Long live the King!

EDMIN:

               . . . I beg you . . . the doctors . . .

MORN:

Enough! I said—tomorrow! Go back, back—   120

in a flying coffin! Yes, in a steel coffin,

on fabricated wings! And what is more:

you said "fairy tale" . . . It makes me laugh . . .

and God laughs with me! The stupefied mob

does not know that the knight's body is dark   125

and sweaty, locked in its fairy-tale armour . . .

VOICE [*quietly*]:

What is it that the King is saying? . . .

MORN:

. . . they do not know that the poor Eastern bride

is barely alive beneath her tasselled weight,

but across the sea the wandering troubadours   130

will sing of a fairy-tale love, will tell lies

to the ages, their fingers barely touching

the sheep sinews—and dirt becomes a dream!

    [*Drinks.*]

VOICE:

What is the King saying?

SECOND VOICE:

He's inebriated! . . .

THIRD VOICE:

135   His eyes shine with madness! . . .

MORN:

Edmin, pour me

some more . . .

LADY [*to the gentleman*]:

Let's go. I am frightened . . .

[. . .]*

[KING]:

A dream once interrupted cannot be resumed,
and the kingdom which sailed before me in a dream
is suddenly revealed as merely standing

140   on the earth. Reality has suddenly intruded.
That, which is flesh and blood, once seemed to glide
like translucent ether; now, suddenly,
stomping like a rough giant, it has entered
into my solid but fragile dream. I see

145   around me the ruins of towers which soared up
to the clouds. Yes, a dream is always
an illusion, all is a lie, a lie.

EDMIN:

She lied

to me too, my sovereign.

KING:

Who lied, Edmin?

[*suddenly remembers*]
Oh, you talk of her? . . . No, my kingdom

150   was an illusion . . . The dream was a lie.
[. . .]*

---

* Lines missing in the original Russian text.

[MORN]:*
Edmin, give it to me! . . . What else should I do?
Fall to my knees? Would you like that? Ah, Edmin,
I must die! I am guilty, not before Ganus,
but before God, before you, before myself,
before my people! I was a bad king: 155
unseen, without courtiers, I ruled by deception . . .
All my power lay in my mysteriousness . . .
The wisdom of my laws? The creativity
and joy of power? The love of the people?
Yes. But empty and deceiving, like the pale jester   160
in his moon-like smock, was the soul of the ruler!
I appeared now in a mask upon the throne,
now in the drawing room of a vain lover . . .
Deception! And my flight was the lie, the trick—
do you hear?—of a coward! And this glory   165
is but the kiss of a blind man . . . Am I
really a king? A king who killed a girl?
No, no, enough, I will fall—to death—
to fiery death! I am but a torch,
thrown into a well, flaming, whirling, flying,   170
flying downwards to meet its reflection,
that grows in the darkness like the dawn . . .
I beg you! I beg you! Give me my black pistol!
You do not speak?
    [*Pause.*]
                Well then, don't . . . There are
other deaths in this world: precipices   175
and maelstroms, poisons and blades, and the knot.
No! You can no more stop a sinner killing
himself, than a genius from being born!

---

*"KING" changes back to "MORN" in the Russian (Azbuka) edition of the play.

[*Pause.*]
But then, I am demeaning myself in vain
180   by these requests . . . A complicated game
with such a simple denouement is boring.
        [*Pause.*]
Edmin, I am your king. Give it to me.
You understand?
        [EDMIN, *without looking, extends the pistol to him.*]
MORN:
                        Thank you. I will go out
onto the terrace. Only the stars will see me.
185   I am happy and lucid; I could not speak
more truthfully . . . Edmin, I'll lightly kiss
your light brow . . . Silence, silence . . . Your
silence is sweeter than any known songs.
So. Thank you.
        [*walks towards the glass door*]
                        The blue night takes me away!
        [*He goes out onto the terrace. His figure, illuminated by the
        night rays, can be seen through the glass door.*]
EDMIN:

190   . . . .
        . . . .

. . . No one must see how
my King presents to the heavens,
the death of Mister Morn.

        CURTAIN

FURTHER READING

The *Tragedy of Mister Morn* was first published in 1997 in *Zvezda*, a Russian literary journal, as "Tragediia Gospodina Morna" ("The Tragedy of Mister Morn"), edited by Serena Vitale and Ellendea Proffer and with an introduction by Vadim Stark (*Zvezda*, no. 4 [1997], pp. 6–98). This translation is based on the play as it subsequently appeared in book form: *Tragediia Gospodina Morna* (St. Petersburg: Azbuka Press, 2008), edited by Andrei Babikov and containing the Russian text of Nabokov's other plays.

Many if not all of Nabokov's other writings cast light on *Morn*. Of especial interest, however, are the early Russian writings, included in the volumes of his collected works in Russian: *Sobranie sochinenii russkogo perioda v piati tomakh* (*Collected Works of the Russian Period in Five Volumes*), with various editors and an introduction to each volume by Alexander Dolinin (St. Petersburg: Symposium, 1999–2000). For readers without Russian, many of Nabokov's other early plays are translated by Dmitri Nabokov in *The Man from the USSR & Other Plays* (San Diego: Bruccoli Clark/Harcourt Brace Jovanovich, 1985), which also contains his important essay on drama, "The Tragedy of Tragedy." Early poems which offer comparisons with *Morn* are translated in Nabokov, *Selected Poems*, edited by Thomas Karshan (New York: Knopf, 2012). Early short stories, many of which bear on *Morn*, are translated in *The Stories of Vladimir Nabokov*

(New York: Knopf, 1995). This last volume contains two short stories, "Ultima Thule" and "Solus Rex," which Nabokov wrote in 1939–40 and which are the only surviving remnants of a novel that would clearly have re-developed the themes of *Morn*. Traces of that project are also to be found in Nabokov's 1947 novel *Bend Sinister*, and still more so in the 1962 *Pale Fire*, the work in which Nabokov most directly re-addressed the images, themes, and ideas of *Morn*.

The definitive biography of Nabokov is the two-volume work by Brian Boyd, whose first volume deals with the period in which Nabokov was writing *Morn* and contains a critical analysis of the play: *Vladimir Nabokov: The Russian Years* (London: Chatto & Windus, 1990). Critical analysis is also offered, for those who read Russian, in Andrei Babikov and Vadim Stark's introductions to their respective editions of *Morn*. Apart from these, there has been little critical analysis of *Morn* to date. Exceptions are: Gennady Barabtarlo, "Nabokov's Trinity: On the Movement of Nabokov's Themes," in *Nabokov and His Fiction: New Perspectives*, edited by Julian Connolly (Cambridge: Cambridge University Press, 1999), pp. 109–38; Siggy Frank, "Exile in Theatre/Theatre in Exile: Nabokov's Early Plays, *Tragediia Gospodina Morna* and *Chelovek iz SSSR*," in the *Slavonic and East European Review*, vol. 85, no. 4 (October 2007), pp. 629–57; A. Iu. Meshchanskii, "'*Tragediia Gospodina Morna*' *kak predtecha russkoiazychnoi prozy V. V. Nabokova*," in *Voprosy filologii*, no. 11 (2002), pp. 100–108; and R. V. Novikov, "'*Tragediia Gospodina Morna*' *V. Nabokova: k poetike 'p'esy-snovideniia,*'" in *Maloizvestnye stranitsy i novye kontseptsii istorii russkoi literatury XX v.: Materialy mezhdunarodnoi nauchnoi konferentsii, Moskva*, edited by L. F. Alekseeva and V. A. Skripkina (Moscow: Moscow State Open University, 2003), pp. 181–87.

Much has been written about Nabokov more generally. Excellent starting points are *The Cambridge Companion to Nabokov*, edited by Julian Connolly (Cambridge: Cambridge University Press, 2005) and the encyclopaedic *Garland Companion to Vladimir Nabokov*, edited by Vladimir Alexandrov (New York: Routledge, 1995). Other recent critical studies include: Vladimir Alexandrov, *Nabokov's Otherworld* (Princeton, NJ: Princeton University Press, 1991); Julian Connolly, *Nabokov's Early Fiction: Patterns of Self and Other* (Cambridge: Cambridge University Press, 1992); Leland de la Durantaye, *Style Is Matter: The Moral Art of Vladimir Nabokov* (Ithaca, NY: Cornell University Press, 2007); Alexander Dolinin, *Istinnaia zhizn' pisatelia Sirina* (St. Petersburg: Academic Project, 2004); Thomas Karshan, *Vladimir Nabokov and the Art of Play* (Oxford: Oxford University Press, 2011); Leona Toker, *Nabokov: The Mystery of Literary Structures* (Ithaca, NY: Cornell University Press, 1989); and Michael Wood, *The Magician's Doubts: Nabokov and the Risks of Fiction* (Princeton, NJ: Princeton University Press, 1995).

A NOTE ABOUT THE AUTHOR

VLADIMIR NABOKOV studied French and Russian literature at Trinity College, Cambridge, then lived in Berlin and Paris, writing prolifically in Russian under the pseudonym Sirin. In 1940, he left France for America, where he wrote some of his greatest works, *Bend Sinister* (1947), *Lolita* (1955), *Pnin* (1957), and *Pale Fire* (1962), and translated his earlier Russian novels into English. He taught at Wellesley, Harvard, and Cornell. He died in Montreux, Switzerland, in 1977.

A NOTE ABOUT THE TRANSLATORS

THOMAS KARSHAN is the author of *Vladimir Nabokov and the Art of Play* and the editor of Nabokov's *Collected Poems*. He is a lecturer in modern literature at the University of East Anglia.

ANASTASIA TOLSTOY is a PhD student at New College, Oxford, where she is writing a thesis on Nabokov and the aesthetics of the Russian emigration.